MW01616743

JEKKA WILDE

QUEEN OF HEARTS

THE WICKED BOYS OF WONDERLAND

BOOK FOUR

Cover design by Wilde & Free LLC

ISBN: 978-1-964291-03-1

CONTENTS

CHAPTER ONE

ALICE

Blinding white light surrounded me, frying my retinas. My nose was filled with the sterile and acrid stench of chemicals and disinfectant spray. My feet were freezing and my lips were cracked and dry. I lay still, either unable or unwilling to move as I blinked against the harsh, bright light from above.

For a moment, I was disoriented, confused by my strange surroundings.

Was I lying outside in the snow that camouflaged the White Queen's castle? Was I in Amari's infirmary, resting on that same cold marble table where Ransom had been not that long ago?

Then it all came flooding back to me.

The asylum.

The padded walls of my room.

The drugs they were pumping into my system to sedate me.

They must've been wearing off. Either that, or I was building up a tolerance.

How did I end up here?

My mind raced as I struggled to remember, but everything was a confusing blur of police officers, and a bunch of people and paparazzi at my favorite Starbucks in Malibu.

Oh . . . that's right . . . I did this to myself.

I'd walked through the giant magic mirror in the training courtyard of Queen Amari's castle and stepped from one world into my own.

I didn't know where I belonged, but it sure as hell wasn't here. I peered through the tiny window in the steel door of my room. The only view was a wall of painted cinderblocks, bathed in the same sickly glow of the buzzing fluorescent lights.

My gaze drifted down, landing on a gooey blue smear on the floor by my bed, and I instantly recoiled. I knew exactly what it was. One of the Red Queen's spies, in the form of a blue worm—a blue pill—had been sent to monitor my every move.

Well . . . it *used* to be a worm.

That motherfucker never stood a chance.

Not when I got through with it.

I hated—absolutely *hated*—that the Red Queen already knew where I was.

How did she know?

I tried to sit up so I could wipe the remaining stain from the floor, and was immediately jerked back down.

"What the hell?"

My eyes slid down to my wrists, then my

ankles . . . which were all held in place by white straps attached somewhere along the bottom of my bed. Another wider band was wrapped around my waist, holding my body down.

The padded walls seemed to pulsate and close in around me as panic rose in my chest. I curled my hands into fists and pulled against the thick, wide straps, but it was useless.

Rage boiled up inside me, white hot, and within mere seconds of spilling over. I wanted to scream . . . to cry. The twisted sound that came out of my throat was a combination of both.

I screamed until my throat was raw.

No one came.

I had to get out of here.

I just *had* to . . . before I actually went insane.

My heart raced as I desperately searched my mind for a solution, a lifeline . . . any scrap of hope to cling to.

I'd been wandering around Wonderland for weeks . . . .maybe longer. There had to be a missing persons report on me by now. So then why didn't the police officers who brought me here mention anything about it?

They couldn't *all* be working for the Red Queen . . .

Could they?

And why hadn't any of my family come to bail me out of this shithole? They'd be appalled if they knew where I was right now.

My parents didn't just have private jet money—we actually owned a private jet. Even if they were in Milan for one of Bianca's fashion shows, or tanning on a beach in Marcella's latest swimwear line, they could've flown home at a moment's notice and made everything better.

Hell . . . if they were that busy, they could've sent one of their attorneys to rescue me instead.

Did my parents and my sisters honestly not notice that I'd been gone all this time?

I ran down the list of names in my head of all the people I'd considered friends . . . and sadly realized they weren't friends at all. They were just shallow assholes that I went to brunch with . . . got my nails done and gossiped with . . . got shitfaced and partied with.

They weren't the type of people you could count on in an actual emergency . . . when a true, dependable friend was needed.

I'd never felt so completely and utterly abandoned in my life.

Abandoned by my family . . .

Abandoned by my friends.

I knew I'd fucked up by not doing my homework about the child labor being used to build my short-lived shoe empire, and yeah, maybe I deserved to be cancelled for like, five minutes, but this was next level bullshit.

It felt like the entire world had abandoned me . . .

At least . . . it felt like *my* world had.

But there was another one that existed parallel to it.

I took a deep breath and thought about the only people I could truly count on.

My wicked boys.

Specifically Jack.

If he could still hear me in his thoughts, there might be hope for me yet. Closing my eyes, I focused all my concentration on Jack, mentally calling out his name. My frantic words trembled with urgency and desperation, echoing through the chaos of my mind.

"Jack . . . I . . . I need you," I stammered into the nothingness. "I d-don't know where I am . . . and I d-don't know how long until they drug me again."

No reply.

Tears began filling my eyes, stinging as they slid down the sides of my face and into my hair.

"Jack . . . are you out there? Can you hear me?"

Suddenly, I felt a spark of recognition, a familiar presence brushing against my consciousness.

Yes, Alice . . . I can hear you. Hold on. It won't be much longer now.

I shuddered at the sound of him speaking in my head as relief washed over me. His voice was strong and determined, full of cool authority and confident reassurance.

"How much longer until you get here?"

No reply.

"Jack?"

Nothing.

"Please . . . don't leave me alone," I begged him, raising my voice in desperation. Maybe this wasn't real. Maybe I was still high on whatever drugs I'd been given. Maybe I was dreaming.

Maybe Jack wasn't even real.

What if none of this was real, and I was trapped in a nightmare? Maybe I'd never found a White Rabbit when I'd left the nightclub in downtown L.A. Maybe I'd been hit by a car and was trapped in a coma, existing somewhere between life and death.

As the minutes ticked by with no reply from Jack, my hopes began to fade into bleak nothingness. I was so alone, trapped in this godforsaken prison with no way out. The darkness threatened to consume me as I lay there, my limbs held down against the cold, hard mattress.

I was spiraling and I knew it, but I couldn't pull myself out of it. I couldn't do anything but lay there and cry as it pulled me down . . .

Down . . .

Down . . .

Further down my own rabbit hole.

I couldn't even wipe the tears from my eyes. Instead, my vision was a blur of salty sorrow and fear.

This place was another level of hell . . . a level I didn't know existed. At least if I'd been in jail, I would've had the chance to talk to someone . . . maybe even make some friends . . . join a gang of other badass babes . . .

But here, locked in this room, it was just me alone

with my thoughts. I wasn't even sure if my family had a clue where I was.

People screamed at all hours of day and night—not that I knew what time it was. There were no clocks, and no windows. There were occasional sandwiches made of mystery meat and a cheese-like product, cups of pudding that had to be eaten with a flimsy plastic spoon.

Someone was moaning and wailing in the distance. Either someone was coming off their meds, or someone was being admitted. Maybe someone was as miserable and confused as I was, and just wanted out of here like I did.

The wailing was followed by a commotion. It sounded like someone had knocked over a chair. I heard raised voices and a louder crash. Then there was yelling and the sound of rushing footsteps down the hall.

I blinked and stared at the tiny window in my door, hoping for a clue about what was going on out there. A nurse and an orderly jogged past my room. Then someone else ran by in scrubs.

"Jack? Is that you?"

Still no response.

If he was coming from Wonderland, it was gonna be a while.

I heard more shouts and then a feral howl.

I'd heard that kind of howl before. Humans weren't supposed to make those sort of sounds, but I'd grown up in Southern California. I'd seen some shit. I sighed and stared up at the caged light fixture anchored to the ceiling.

Sounds like someone's strung out on meth or fentanyl . . . I hope I'm not getting a new roommate.

It wasn't until I heard the familiar beep of my door being unlocked that I realized how much trouble I was in. The door opened and two men in lab coats stepped through it without making a sound. One of them covered my window with something and quietly shut the door while the taller one slipped his security card into a pocket and stepped closer to me.

This wasn't a normal visit. It didn't take two doctors to give me my medicine. It didn't even take one. It was always a nurse who shot me full of drugs.

And they never covered the window when they sedated me.

Fuck.

It was hard to see the doctor's features through my tears, but I could tell he had dark hair and a thick-framed pair of glasses. He shared a glance with the other doctor before studying the restraints holding me down.

Then his mouth spread wide.

It wasn't a kind, sweet smile, either.

It was sinister as fuck.

My heart sank.

There was absolutely no way for me to defend myself from what was about to happen.

"No . . . " I warned, twisting away from him as best as I could. "Don't!"

The shorter, lighter haired doctor walked over to the other side of my bed, adjusting the stethoscope draped over his broad shoulders. I blinked furiously, trying to register his expression through my blurry tears.

But I couldn't read a thing.

All I could feel was restrained fury . . . tempered rage for what was about to happen next.

I strained against the cuffs holding my arms and legs down, helpless to stop the two doctors from what they were about to do to me . . . desperately wishing there was more between us than my flimsy cotton hospital gown and a pair of fuzzy socks.

"What a shame to waste such a perfect opportunity," the doctor in glasses said to me. He reached down and trailed a warm finger along the inside of my bare calf. I steeled myself, ready to fight however I could. "It's not every day that I find one of my bunnies caught in someone else's snare."

If I hadn't been strapped down to my bed, I would've jumped right out of it.

I couldn't believe what I was hearing. My eyes widened as I watched the doctor slip off his glasses and lean down closer.

"Ransom?"

He grinned wider, his dark eyes simmering with power.

"Hello, my naughty bunny," he murmured, his voice low and husky. His eyes roamed my body, a hint of desire flickering within their depths. A sly grin appeared on his face, and his brow lifted with mischief. "Miss us?"

"More than you know, my king," I replied, my voice thick with emotion.

"That's what I wanted to hear," he said, clearly pleased that I'd remembered to call him by his title. "Be a good girl for me and hold still. We wouldn't want you to get hurt."

My eyes darted down to the other doctor, who'd reached under his white lab coat and pulled out a dagger.

My heart started racing.

"What are you doing?" I hissed, my voice trembling.

"Freeing you from this hideous contraption," Jack replied coolly, his voice like velvet. My heart practically burst out of my chest at the sound of it. At the sound of *both* of their voices.

I whimpered at the sensation of cold steel sliding between the restraints and my ankles, then my wrists. Then it crept along my gown, teasing my belly and my ribs . . .

Even though I was trapped in the asylum, I felt a familiar ache in my pussy at the mere touch of Jack's deadly blade.

At the sound of Ransom calling me his bunny.

Jack quickly sliced through the restraints holding me down, then slipped the dagger back in place. I barely had time to rub my eyes before he was scooping me up in his powerful arms. I held him tight, clinging to him for dear life, breathing in his smell of wild forests, of balsam and smoke and sweat.

"I can't believe I didn't recognize you," I sighed as I lifted my head and took a good look at him.

His long, pale hair was neatly combed back into a low ponytail, and his jawline was rough with the slightest bit of scruff. He was still my White Knight . . . he'd simply traded the horned helmet and sinister platinum armor for a white lab coat.

I let my fingers trace the shape of the stethoscope around his neck as I gazed into his glittering red eyes.

"You came . . . "

"I told you I would," he said. The intensity of his gaze didn't waver for a second.

My heart was doing flip-flops, and I was doing everything I could not to get emotional and say something stupid.

"If all my doctors looked like you guys, I would've tried to get sick more often."

"We could play doctor sometime, if you'd like," Ransom snickered as Jack set me down. He took out his key card, flipping it along his nimble fingers, doing tricks he must've learned from spending eternity inside a casino.

"You two can play later," Jack said while dragging a wheelchair over to me. "Have a seat, Alice. Your chariot awaits."

Ransom pushed open the door while Jack steered my little chariot. I was grateful to be sitting because my knees were shaking with gratitude.

The shouting and commotion grew louder as we

went down the hall. The elevator came into view, then the windows as I was rolled into what seemed to be a community room.

It was dark outside, and I could see the lights of Los Angeles stretch to the edge of the horizon. We must've been up at least ten stories.

There were no patients milling about like I expected. A nearby clock on the wall told me it was one twenty-three in the morning. That explained why. But it didn't explain the reason the clerk at the front desk was hiding behind the safety of the shatter-proof glass that surrounded it.

A chair flew past the cubicle and bounced off the glass, and I instantly realized what the problem was.

The asylum staff was in an uproar, trying to tame the chaos that was raining down all around us. I heard a gleeful, yet completely maniacal laugh, and I immediately recognized who it was coming from.

Hatter.

Of course it was Hatter.

Classic Hatter.

He was jumping from one piece of furniture to another, his top hat wobbling, yet somehow never falling from his head. His one bright blue eye was glowing with delight, and I couldn't help wondering if this was exactly what he was meant for.

"Many mumbling mice . . . are making merry music in the moonlight . . . " he sang, before belting out, "MIGHTY NICE!"

Then he went up and octave, and sang it again.

"Many mumbling mice are making merry music in the moonlight . . . MIGHTY NICE!"

His wild eyes met mine, and his grin stretched almost across his entire face, revealing most of his teeth, before he sang his song again, still one octave higher than before.

"MANY MUMBLING MICE . . . " he practically flew out of the grasp of three orderlies, bounding around the room like a feral creature.

But then . . . he *was* the Mad Hatter. I was pretty sure that being a feral creature was in his DNA.

"Let's get you out of here, shall we?" Ransom suggested before ushering Jack towards the elevator.

"I don't need to be asked twice," I choked. I could barely speak. Yeah, my voice was hoarse from screaming, but there was also a massive lump in my throat. I'm sure it was caused by my heart swelling with adoration for these men who had managed to escape Wonderland, and break into a locked-down facility and rescue me.

Their loyalty and devotion fueled my hope, igniting a fire within me that burned away the tendrils of despair. I had no idea what they were risking by coming here, although now wasn't the time to ask.

Now was the time to play my part, to be a good girl, keep calm, let my 'doctors' push me into the elevator, and take me far, far away from this nightmare.

Office supplies and papers were flying around the room, magically being sucked through the small opening in the shatterproof glass around the main desk. Hatter dodged a stapler and it went flying into an orderly's forehead.

The wild performance was working perfectly to divert the staff's attention as Ransom pushed the button to the ground floor. Hatter jumped onto tables, still spouted nonsensical rhymes, and threw a tea set across the room. The orderlies scrambled through the broken ceramic to catch him, but his agility kept them at bay.

"Is Hatter going to be okay?" I asked, concern lacing my voice as the doors sealed us inside.

"Trust me, Alice," Ransom reassured, a wicked smirk playing on his lips. "Hatter will be just fine. Let's get you into a proper getaway outfit, shall we?"

He waved his hand in a fluid 'S' shape, and my flimsy cotton hospital gown was replaced by a skin-tight black cocktail dress made of lace that resembled spider webs.

Then I glanced at my feet, and snorted a laugh.

I was still wearing the ugly fuzzy socks.

"Maybe something less formal?" I politely suggested. I stared at my feet, imagining myself wearing a pair of white sneakers, but nothing happened.

The magic of my imagination that had become so easy to use in Wonderland had disappeared here.

"What about this?" Ransom asked. Suddenly I was wearing my favorite Balenciaga sweatshirt, the striped Gucci track pants I'd imagined from Net-a-Porter, and my Uggs.

"I could fucking kiss you right now," I groaned as I settled into my beloved cozies.

"No time for that," Jack said as the elevator came to a stop. "We have to get out of here as quickly as possible."

He lifted me out of the chair and the three of us headed for the nearest exit. The moment the doors opened to the soft night air, I breathed a sigh of relief. The last traces of the acrid disinfectant smell were replaced with the smell of car exhaust and a 24-hour donut shop.

A helicopter hummed in the distance, and a car drove by, thumping bass so hard that the windows rattled. I was never so grateful to be free to move about the city.

A black luxury convertible was parked alongside the curb, its motor humming quietly. Jack helped me into the passenger seat so gently that I wondered if he thought my bones were broken.

I didn't mind being babied a little.

Not by him.

After what I'd been through, I kinda loved it.

I took a deep breath of the supple leather and ran my fingers along the interior of my upgraded chariot. Judging by the black leather seats and gold accents, I knew who the manufacturer was.

Not Lotus, or McLaren.

Not Lamborghini.

No . . . the emblem on the hood was a gold rabbit, just like the one on the doors of the Rabbit Hole Casino, and I knew the car maker was Ransom.

Was there anything he *couldn't* do?

It turned out there was.

Apparently, he couldn't drive.

I lifted a curious eyebrow as Jack pulled off his white lab coat to reveal not medieval monster armor, but a slim cut dark blue sweater and perfectly tailored grey chinos. I felt an ache of longing as I watched him settle his toned ass behind the wheel.

"You know how to drive?"

He shot me a stern look. Then his face softened.

"Of course I do. I'm not from Wonderland. I was born in France."

"Yeah, but that was like . . . a really long time ago, wasn't it?"

Jack shrugged, then put the car in reverse.

"I *do* take holidays. Where do you think I go?"

I didn't have time to answer. My body flew forward as he slammed on the gas, propelling the three of us backwards faster than my body had ever moved in my life. I was just about to scream at Jack for driving like a maniac when I heard the sound of a *true* maniac shrieking from above.

I looked up into the night sky to see a glittering shower of stars above us. For some weird reason, they were getting bigger and bigger.

Fuck.

Those weren't stars.

They were shards of broken glass rocketing towards us as fast as gravity would let them. And there, in the middle of it all, was Hatter, flailing and laughing as he fell from at least ten stories above.

I screamed and ducked my head down between my knees, burying it in my arms. I was trying to yell at Jack to drive. All that came out was, "AAAAAGGGHHHH!"

Glass was falling down all around us, hitting the pavement like bright, twinkling, happy notes of music. I felt something heavy land in the seat behind me. Suddenly my back was pinned to my seat as Jack revved the engine and peeled out of the parking lot.

CHAPTER TWO

ALICE

My body lurched from side to side as Jack sped through intersections and weaved effortlessly around the vehicles on the road. Wind whipped my long hair around so hard that the chunks of glass had been flung right out of it.

"Where am I going?" he asked nonchalantly.

"How the hell should I know?" I shot back in exasperation. "I thought you guys had a plan!"

"The plan was to rescue you from your prison, and we did that," Hatter explained from the seat behind me. "Do we need another plan?"

I rolled my eyes and immediately regretted it when strands of hair got caught in them. Wrangling it as best as I could, I got busy putting it into a braid before it got too tangled.

"We should probably make another plan," Ransom agreed. "Alice, what do you want more than anything right now?"

"Tacos," I blurted out, not missing a beat. "And then I wanna go home and take a long bath."

Hatter gave Ransom a confused glance before focusing his attention on me.

"What?" I shrugged. "I'm hungry!"

"So . . . tacos are food?" Hatter asked.

"They're the *best* food," I told him. "We can't leave the city until you try them."

"Very well," Ransom declared. "We'll procure tacos and go to your house. That's the new plan. I'll catch up with you."

Out of the corner of my eye, I saw him grasp the back of Jack's seat and pull himself forward.

Then he stood up . . . while the convertible was still cruising down the boulevard. Jack's driving had slowed down to the speed limit, but I was still wearing my seat belt.

"What the—"

I gasped as Ransom shot up into the air as his leathery black wings exploded through the back of his suit jacket. Neon lights illuminated the entire length of his fully outstretched wingspan. His powerful wings beat a few times, propelling him up into the dark sky.

I couldn't help feeling a deep sense of awe mixed with a little fear at the sight of him soaring away. With my jaw practically sitting in my lap, I turned to Jack.

"Where the fuck did he go?"

"I assume he went to find tacos." Jack came to a

stoplight and turned to me. "Can you instruct me how to get to your house?"

"It's west of the city. In Malibu."

"Could you be more specific?"

I nodded. "Sure. Take a right at the next light and get on the highway."

While Jack navigated the streets of Los Angeles and headed for the hills, I flicked a piece of glass off my lap and relaxed into my cushy leather seat.

Never, ever, once in my wildest dreams had I imagined my wicked boys existing anywhere else outside of Wonderland. Of all the places they could've found themselves, L.A. was one of the better options. I doubted anyone had even noticed a literal demon jumping out of a convertible and flying away in search of tacos.

And if they *had* noticed, I bet they didn't think too much of it.

As we sped along the Pacific Coast Highway, the full moon sank closer to the horizon, casting its silvery glow over the ocean on our left, its reflection shimmering like liquid diamonds on the inky black waves.

The further Jack, Hatter, and I drove from the city, the darker the sky became and the brighter the stars shined.

This wasn't a dream.

This was as real as the wind whipping through my hair.

The salty air filled my lungs, cleansing me of the last traces of that sterile hospital scent that clung to my skin. My White Knight had rescued me, and was whisking me off to safety. The Mad Hatter and Ransom were his partners in crime.

But what about my other wicked, wonderful boys?

I bit my lip before remembering that this was my king's job, not mine. And because I wasn't one to shy away from confrontation, I tilted my head and gave the White Knight a curious look.

"Why didn't Chess and Callister want to join your rescue mission?"

"Chess wanted to, but he was outvoted. Callister thought it was best for him to stay and get a head start on creating ambushes for the Red Queen's army," Jack replied.

Hatter let out an amused laugh.

"I doubt the Caterpillar would've been much help in your rescue, if you ask me."

I twisted around and saw him laying stretched out across the entire length of the backseat. His long fae legs were propped up on one edge of the car while he rested his head on the other side. His top hat rested safely on his chest, held in place with a strong hand to keep it from blowing away.

The wind toyed with his blue hair, making him look wilder than ever. I thought about climbing back there and fucking him under the moonlight . . . wind blasting in our faces as we howled at the night sky.

But I had questions.

"Why don't you think Callister would've been helpful tonight? He knows how to fight."

Hatter shook his head.

"He's gotten weak. If he managed to land a punch, it wouldn't leave so much as a bruise."

"Hatter . . . " Jack growled in a warning tone.

"Oh, stop. Alice isn't going to run and tell the Red Queen. She's going to find out soon enough."

My eyes widened with worry.

"Find out about what? Is Callister okay? What's wrong with him?"

"Nothing's wrong with him," Hatter said, waving a dismissive hand. "Nothing's wrong with him at all. Everything is exactly as it should be."

I frowned in confusion. "I don't understand."

"He's about to go through his metamorphosis," Jack said from the driver's seat. "Once he sheds his skin, he'll be fine."

"Until that time, he'll be a downright fright," Hatter sang. "A downright fright alright. And even though he's lost all his muscle and might, I wouldn't want to face him in the deep dark night. His skin is all saggy and his flesh is drawn tight. What a horrific sight!"

I stared at Hatter for a few silent seconds, taking in his wacky song. Then I turned back to Jack.

"How can you say there's nothing wrong with Callister? It sounds like he's in really bad shape."

"It's normal. He'll be fine. Watch your head, Alice. We have incoming."

"Huh?"

I looked up just in time to scream at the horrifying, giant bat-monster descending upon us at break-neck speed. Jack didn't even step on the brakes, let alone flinch, as Ransom landed in the backseat with a thud—directly on top of Hatter.

"My silk top hat! You squished it flat!" he howled in indignation.

"Serves you right for taking up both seats," Ransom laughed from behind as he thrust a grease-stained brown bag into my lap.

"That one's all yours, bunny. I have another bag for us to share back here."

An *entire* bag of tacos?

Just for *me*?

It didn't matter that Ransom had never said he loved me.

That was love, right there.

My mouth immediately began to water as I dug into the bag and lifted out a piping hot street taco. With my mouth full of corn tortilla and fillings, I offered a bite to Jack.

His eyes flicked over to me, and he shook his head.

"I already ate," he said in a cryptic tone, his gaze never leaving the road. The full moon illuminated his sharp profile, shadows clinging to his high cheekbones. "How much further to your house?"

"We're almost there," I said with my mouth full. My heart thudded with anticipation of what would he would do to me when we got there. Jack had never mentioned if he cared that I was fucking his friends. I didn't know if he was the jealous, possessive type.

What if he wanted me all to himself?

I couldn't think about that right now. Instead, I shoved the last bit of carne asada into my mouth. I only stopped eating to rattle off the directions to my house. My words tumbled over each other in my impatience and nervousness.

"Turn right at the sign, then follow the winding road up the hills. The gates will be locked, but I have the code. You can't miss it."

Jack rolled through the stop sign, then took a hard right. The dark Pacific stretched endlessly behind us, the waves making the moonlight sparkle. The salty breeze caressed my skin, and I realized something . . .

I didn't remember the last time I was this happy.

Like . . . genuinely happy to just be alive in this moment in time.

After weeks locked away in that miserable room, secured to that uncomfortable bed, freedom was so close that I could taste it through the crumbled Cotija cheese.

And I was with my wicked boys of Wonderland.

Jack sped up the winding hillside road, and slowly, my house came into view. Landscape lighting illuminated the exterior from the windows onto the sprawling deck, but the driveway was empty. We would have the house to ourselves tonight.

To be fair, it *was* two-thirty in the morning.

But if you had paparazzi driving by your house at all hours of the day and night, you'd be just as relieved.

"Home sweet home," I murmured as we approached the gates to my house. Punching in the security code, I sighed in relief, reveling in the familiar sounds and scents of home, and drinking in the sight of my beloved sanctuary.

Tonight, there would be no doctors, no nurses, no guards.

Just me and the people who truly mattered.

The ones who had risked everything to set me free.

Jack pulled up to the front door, and I jumped out of the car the second he shut off the engine. I ran to the front door and punched in another security code, but Jack grabbed my shoulders and held me tight, stopping me from making it past the entryway.

I looked up at him, wondering if he wanted an actual hug.

"Wait until we've searched the house."

Even though I knew he might have a point, my heart sank.

I just wanted him to want me.

And right now, he seemed oblivious to what I thought was an obvious desire.

"It won't take long. Hatter, stay down here with Alice while we search the house."

We watched Jack and Ransom disappear in opposite directions, switching on lights and moving from room to room so quickly that all I saw were their dark, blurry shadows.

I didn't even have time to ask Hatter what he thought about the tacos before he swept me into his arms, lifting me up and spinning me around until I was dizzy and breathless.

"Did you miss me? Because I certainly missed you."

"Of course I missed you," I sighed into his warm neck. "I'm so glad you're here."

He set me down, took my hand, and led me towards the kitchen.

"Seems a shame to have such a grand mansion and not have anyone in it."

"There's people here during the day," I replied. "The cleaners and my grocery deliveries come on Mondays, the gardeners are here on Wednesdays, and the pool guy stops by every Thursday."

Hatter quirked an eyebrow at me while shaking his head.

"Are they here because they want to be?"

"If they wanna get paid, they are." I grabbed a few glasses from the cabinet and set them out, then opened the fridge. It was perfectly stocked, just the way I liked it. I spotted a container of fresh strawberries that had been washed and ready to eat. I grabbed them and a bottle of orange juice, then shut the door.

Hatter's arms were folded across his chest.

"Don't you have friends? What about your family? Don't you have parties where this massive house is filled to the gills with people who love and adore you?"

His words cut like a cold knife, slicing so deep that I almost dropped the orange juice. My eyes began to sting, and I focused all my attention on filling two glasses. I handed him one to shut him up, and sipped on mine to buy myself some time.

"I only bought this place because it'll have a great resale value," I said, trying to sound breezy and unbothered by his earlier comment.

But the truth was that I couldn't remember the last time I'd had a party . . . like, an actual blowout bash. It was probably my housewarming party, back before I'd done any remodeling.

I didn't remember anything about that night.

Although . . . I *did* remember that nobody stayed long enough to help clean up the disaster that was left when it was over. That's what the cleaners were hired to do.

They weren't hired to care about me. Just take care of me . . .

"All clear," Ransom announced as he and Jack strolled into the kitchen. "I'm going to make some drinks. Want one, Alice?"

I gave him a tight, yet grateful smile.

"Yeah, that would be great."

Ignoring the concern on Jack's face, I hustled as fast as I could up the stairs, making a beeline for my private bathroom.

Slamming the door behind me, I sank onto the heated tile floor and burst into tears.

I wasn't a crybaby, but something about Hatter's words just pushed me over the edge.

He wasn't wrong about his observations. What was the point of having this huge house if the only people who came over were on my payroll? Sure, I had a fridge full of groceries and a stunning pool and immaculate landscaping, but there was nobody to share it with.

My sisters and parents were too busy with their own lives to get involved in mine.

My friends were always the ones inviting me to parties, clubs, and other events. I always had to go to wherever they were, or give them a ride, or pay for the cabs, the checks, the cover charges, and the VIP sections. I'd always thought of myself as the leader of the pack, so I felt obligated to pay for everything.

But aside from my housewarming party, not one of my so-called friends had ever come out to my house to hang out.

Not once.

And now there were three men in my kitchen. Three men who'd busted me out of the insane asylum and brought me to safety.

And they'd brought me tacos.

Nobody else in my life would've done that for me.

They deserved to see me at my best, not see me sad and crying.

I had to clean myself up and get my shit together.

I had to do it for them. And for myself.

I wiped my eyes and looked around. Everything appeared just about the way I'd left it, although I could tell that the cleaners had been through at some point. The trash can was empty and the toilet paper had the neat fold in it like you saw at nicer hotels . . . until I tore off a bit and used it.

My bathtub was calling to me, beckoning like a

high-class escort to a lonely traveling businessman at an expensive hotel. I imagined the tub filled with hot water and suds.

Nothing happened.

Wonderland had spoiled me.

I shook my head and leaned over to turn on the faucet, then found the bubble bath mix and poured in a generous amount. After tossing in a bath bomb, I dimmed the lights, peeled off my clothes, and climbed into the steaming water filling my oversized bathtub.

My head rested against a waterproof cushion and I watched little mountains of frothy bubbles pile up all around me. Their soft scent quickly enveloped me in a warm embrace.

I needed this—to wash away the lingering taint of the asylum . . . the horrible feeling of being held captive . . . of having no control over what happened to me. The fear leached out of my bones and drifted away with the steam that was starting to fog up the window beside me.

There was a soft, firm knock at the door that startled me out of my thoughts.

"Alice, are you alright?" Jack asked from the other side, his tone tinged with concern. His protective nature never ceased to amaze me, and I couldn't help but smile at his thoughtfulness. "I've brought your drink."

"I'm fine. Come on in."

He slipped through the door, then glanced away after catching sight of me in the tub.

"I didn't realize . . . " he said with tender modesty, still keeping his gaze averted while handing me my drink. "I'll leave you to your bath."

"No. Stay."

I swallowed a mouthful of my cocktail, savoring how the alcohol burned pleasantly down my throat. I groaned in satisfaction, relishing the burst of sweet and tangy flavors on my tongue. After only having bland food and plain water in the asylum, this incubus-made beverage was sheer ambrosia.

"You're not fine," Jack said, leaning against the countertop. "I can tell you've been crying."

I took another gulp of my cocktail, then looked at the White Knight.

"I'm better now that you're here. Aren't you warm in that sweater?"

Jack shook his head.

"You know that I'm rarely warm no matter what I wear."

"Let me feel your hands," I told him, beckoning him over. He outstretched his arm, offering me his upright palm. A flicker of heat lit up in his dark red eyes, but he was right—his hand was cool to the touch.

"Damn! Your skin is like ice! Maybe you should get in with me and warm up," I suggested with a flirtatious smile.

Jack's eyes narrowed, and I could see the hunger beginning to bloom inside of him.

"If I join you in the bath, we both know how that's going to end up."

"Oh yeah? How's that?" I teased.

Jack shot me a wicked snarl.

"With me inside you."

Using my arm like a giant shovel, I ran it along the surface of the water and scooped away all the bubbles that were obstructing Jack's view from my waist down. I lifted my right ankle and draped it over the edge of the tub, giving him an excellent view of my pussy.

"Then what are you waiting for?"

The muscles in Jack's jaw feathered as his eyes traced the lines of my body beneath the water. It was the only part of his body that stirred.

"Unlike you, I'm capable of showing restraint, Alice," he said with an arrogant expression. "I'm not going to fuck you when you've just been freed from your prison . . . when you've been crying. When you're upset. My cock isn't an emotional crutch. Furthermore . . . you've been drinking."

I pursed my lips at his words.

Was this a challenge?

Challenge accepted.

"Fine. Don't fuck me," I shrugged as I slipped my leg back under the water and set my glass aside. "You can still get in and warm up with me. And just for the record, I've only had half a drink. I could recite the alphabet backwards if you wanted me to."

Jack didn't move.

I lifted a brow, grinning at him.

"Do you actually want me to recite the alphabet backwards?"

"No."

"Then what's wrong?"

"Nothing's wrong," he murmured.

I wasn't buying it.

"Don't you think you can be naked in a bath with me and not fuck me?"

"I can . . . " he said slowly.

"Prove it."

The haughty arrogance in Jack's beautiful face was turning me on, and I didn't care if he could sense it or not. If he wanted to be nosy and read my thoughts, then he'd have to get used to the fact that I found him insanely attractive, whether he was wearing leather armor, or a cashmere sweater with slim-cut pants.

For a moment, it felt like Jack was considering whether or not to turn around and walk out of the bathroom.

But he wasn't just a man.

He was a vampire.

The temptation of my warm body would be too much for him to resist. Especially when he'd come all this way to rescue me.

Slowly, his hands crept down to the hem of his sweater, then the shirt tucked underneath. I watched his fingers curl around the fabric and gently lift it up his abdomen, then over his head. He kept his movements slow and deliberate, his deadly gaze never leaving mine.

What a fucking tease.

His pale, muscular body was bathed in the glow

of the dimmed lights. The sight of him was breathtaking, and I couldn't help but drink in every inch of his chiseled form as he elegantly pulled out the tie that held back his long hair. A platinum cascade tumbled down past his collarbones, brushing against flawless skin.

His broad shoulders tapered down to a trim waist, while his powerful thighs hinted at the strength hidden within them. His cock lay in a bed of light blond curls, a sleeping giant that I was hell-bent on waking up.

"Come here," I murmured, my voice heavy with desire. Jack hesitated only briefly before slipping into the tub and settling himself beneath me. Our bodies melted together, the hot water and fragrant bubbles enveloping us like a silken cocoon. As his arms wrapped around my waist, I tilted my head back to meet his gaze, my eyes brimming with unspoken emotion.

"Thanks for saving me," I breathed, before pulling him in for a searing kiss. His lips pressed against mine, tender and yet filled with a desperate urgency that echoed my own need. Our tongues danced together, exploring and teasing as we clung to one another—two souls bound by blood.

"Dammit, Alice," Jack groaned, his hands roaming my body with a feverish intensity. "I thought we'd lost you. Why did you leave us without any warning?"

I instinctively glanced away, not wanting to answer him. Heat flooded my cheeks as I stared determinedly at the surface of the water, acutely aware of his proximity to my thoughts.

A finger curled under my chin, tilting my face up to the monster who possessed my body . . . and my heart. "There's no need to be shy, Alice." Jack's lips curved into a gentle smile. "Not after everything we've shared."

"Just kiss me," I breathed against his lips, but he backed away before I could taste them again.

"Not until you answer my question." His voice was rough with authority. The kind of authority it took to command the White Queen's army. "Why did you leave us? I know your frustration with Amari wasn't the only reason."

"If you already know the reason, then why do you need me to say it out loud?"

The weight of Jack's gaze surrounded me, heavy and hungry and quietly demanding.

"I want you to say it because I deserve to hear it."

I bit my lip and looked away, realizing that I was more comfortable having Jack bite me and drink my blood than I was with being honest about my feelings.

But as I recalled my time in the asylum, staring at nothing and feeling so lost and empty, I knew I couldn't let him slip out of my life again.

"I left because . . . because I didn't think you guys cared about me," I stammered before I lost my nerve. "At least, not as much as I was starting to care about you."

Jack responded with a barely perceptible nod. "You were afraid. You ran."

"Yeah."

His gaze darkened.

"But I am a hunter. And I caught you."

I tilted my face up to his.

"I was so afraid I'd never see you again," I said softly. "When I ended up in the asylum, locked away and strapped down to a bed . . . " I shook my head. "I realized I'd made a horrible mistake. It nearly destroyed me. I can't lose you guys again."

"You won't. I'm here now . . . *we're* here now, and we're not going anywhere without you." He traced the line of my jaw with his cool fingertips, and I couldn't help marveling at how soothing it felt. "You belong to us, Alice. Nothing will change that fact."

My heart flipped in my chest. "Is that so?"

"Yes. I can't speak for the others, but you and I are bonded, remember? Heart, body and soul. Forever."

"Forever," I echoed, my voice barely above a whisper. He lowered his head to capture my mouth in a kiss that left me breathless. By the time he pulled away, desire had reignited in my veins, hot and insistent.

As our kiss deepened, Jack's hands roamed over my body beneath the water, igniting sparks of pleasure wherever he touched. I arched into his caress, craving more of his addictive touch.

When his lips traveled down my neck, I tilted my head back with a soft moan. His teeth grazed my throat, sharp and tantalizing, sending a thrill of anticipation through me. His vampire bite was a symbol of the profound bond we now shared, and the memory of that exquisite pain and pleasure still made me shiver with delight.

I tangled my hands in Jack's wet hair, pressing him closer in a silent plea. He seemed to understand, his kisses turning hungrier, more demanding. His hands gripped my hips as he lifted me to straddle his lap, the hard length of his cock splitting my pussy lips apart.

Our gazes locked, dark blue meeting blood-red, and in Jack's eyes I saw a level of devotion as deep and endless as the sea.

"I thought you said you weren't gonna fuck me," I taunted.

"I changed my mind," he growled.

Without warning, Jack thrust deep inside me. I cried out at the sudden invasion, bracing my hands on his shoulders. My inner walls clenched around him as sparks of pleasure ignited within me.

Jack groaned, his fingers digging into my hips hard enough to bruise as he began to roll his body against mine. His strokes were forceful and demanding, pushing me rapidly toward the edge of climax. I rocked my hips to meet his thrusts, craving the sweet ache and stretch of his possession.

The water sloshed over the sides of the tub as our passion mounted, but I was too lost in the spiral of pleasure to notice, let alone give a shit. Jack pounded into me relentlessly, hitting that perfect spot deep inside on every stroke.

My release was hurtling toward me, an oncoming

storm that threatened to shatter me into a million pieces. Just when I thought I couldn't take any more, Jack latched onto my throat and pierced the skin with his fangs.

The pain of his bite faded into ecstasy, his rhythmic strokes driving me higher and higher as he rode me mercilessly. I clung to him, barely aware of my fingernails digging into his back like claws, scoring his pale skin.

Jack growled against my throat, fucking me harder. His skin heated under my touch until it was nearly scalding, the fire seeming to race through my veins with every beat of my heart.

The dual sensations of hard pain and soft euphoria tipped me over the edge . . . straight into an orgasm like nothing I'd experienced before. Jack's name was a scream on my lips as rapture tore through my body, intensified by the erotic pull at my neck as he sucked me and drank me.

My inner walls clamped down on Jack's length, dragging him with me into the whirlwind of pleasure. I screamed as I came apart again and again, the force of it shattering what was left of my control.

He stiffened against my body, his climax triggering another wave of ecstasy as he emptied himself inside me. He took one last mouthful from my neck, then licked the wound clean before healing it with a few drops of his own blood.

We clung to each other, trembling from the force of our release and the incredible intimacy of sharing both our blood and our bodies. I nestled into the warmth of Jack's embrace, sated and content. His hands stroked slow circles over my back as we lay in a tangle of limbs, the water lapping gently around us.

At long last, he was warm.

So warm.

And he was mine.

CHAPTER THREE

RANSOM

I awoke in a mess of muscular limbs and dirty sheets, the remnants of last night's indulgence lingering on my skin and in the air. My body hummed with renewed vigor, my incubus energy replenished by the feast of lust and desire that had consumed the three of us.

Hatter stirred on the other side of our shared lover, his beautiful fae features made even more ethereal by his sleepy satisfaction. Our gazes met across the curved landscape of human flesh between us, our lust-hazed minds burning with the memories of the night before.

My cock twitched as I recalled the three of us writhing together, our bodies moving as one, with Alice caught between us as we brought her to one climax after another.

My bunny had done so well. Made me so fucking proud.

She might've fucked the White Knight before coming to us, but I was still her king.

Last night, she had been an insatiable force, her hunger for both of us seemingly endless. I couldn't blame her, not when we were so uniquely suited to fulfill each other's desires.

I'd have to thank Jack for doing such an outstanding job of warming her up.

While he didn't care to partake in group activities, he certainly didn't seem to mind sharing Alice with us.

Not that he'd have a choice.

When it came to Alice, we had to share, or go without.

And none of us were willing to go without her . . . to exist without her. That's why we'd come along to rescue her in the first place.

She was *ours*.

Now she lay between us, her eyes heavy with deep, deep sleep, yet a smirk still lingered on her swollen pink lips.

The world outside the bedroom window had shifted, the light of morning seeping through the cracks in the curtains, the start of a new day dawning. We had much to discuss, plans to make, and alliances to forge.

But for now, I inhaled the rich scent of Alice's arousal mingling with ours, the perfume of our communion clinging to my skin. The night had been everything I'd fantasized about and more, a feast for all my senses.

And yet, I was still hungry for more.

Hatter's warm fingers caressed my forearm, a silent question in his mismatched eyes.

I knew exactly what he was thinking.

I was thinking it as well.

I nodded at our shared understanding, my eyes only leaving Alice's peaceful face for a second. The unspoken agreement between Hatter and I solidified. We extricated ourselves from her unconscious embrace and pulled back the covers. Her naked body was a tableau of sensual abandonment on the rumpled sheets.

She was ours for the taking.

Ours to ruin.

And she would love every moment of it.

"Hatter, would you be a dear and spread her legs?" I quietly asked, my voice dripping with lust and satisfaction.

He didn't hesitate, his eyes alight with hunger as he gently parted her thighs, revealing her wet, pouting pussy. Alice moaned in her sleep, her back softly arching as if she could feel our gaze on her. My demon cock throbbed in anticipation.

"Good . . . very good. Now taste her."

As Hatter leaned down to take a closer look at Alice's exposed cunt, I could see his arousal written across his face. He dipped down his head, letting his tongue delicately trace a line of fire up Alice's inner thigh, his lips teasing her skin with featherlight kisses. Alice moaned again, her hips shifting against the bed in response to his touch, yet she remained asleep.

Her arousal was palpable, the scent of her desire filling the room and making my demon blood boil. My hand skirted along my body until I was grasping my cock. As a creature who fed on sexual energy, I'd developed an appetite for the uncommon.

Not that standard missionary position wasn't enjoyable.

It was . . . but it was more of an appetizer.

Watching my bad little bunny be licked into wailing, mind-shattering consciousness was akin to a seven-course meal.

And I was *hungry*.

Hatter licked his lips in anticipation before plunging into Alice's warm folds. I watched with voyeuristic delight as he expertly licked and sucked at her clit, coaxing out moans from her sleep-slackened mouth. My own cock twitched in response as I stroked it, eager to join in the feast.

My turn would come.

For now, I let Hatter have his fill of Alice. He had waited just as long as I had for this moment, after all. I watched him lap at her gash, then lift his head, savoring the taste of her on his tongue before going back for more.

I closed my hand tighter around my length, pumping it in time with Hatter's tongue as it continued stroking Alice's sensitive flesh.

Heat coiled in my belly at the memory of her flavor. I imagined it was me nestled between her thighs, me dragging my tongue through her slick heat before lapping her juices and sucking on her clit.

Letting go of my hard cock, I moved closer to them, my fingers trailing lightly over Hatter's back before reaching over to caress Alice's breasts. They were soft and warm under my touch, her nipples hardening under my ministrations.

While I sucked on her soft, supple tits, I watched from the corner of my eye as Hatter's tongue slid out of Alice's cunt. He rose up on his knees and gazed down at her sleeping form.

A growl rumbled in my chest as he spread Alice's limp legs even wider. Her cunt was a swollen, shiny, wet temptress, calling to us.

Begging to be filled.

"Fuck her," I rasped. "Look how badly she needs you."

Hatter's fingers wandered over Alice's body, physically admiring every curve, responding to every subtle shift of her body while she slept.

"Look at that," he murmured, tracing a finger along her swollen folds. "So wet and ready for me. But I shouldn't..."

My hand sped up on my cock, twisting on every stroke. I was desperate to watch him mount her, to watch him satisfy the desire burning within us all.

The anticipation threatened to overwhelm me, but I held on through sheer force of will, determined that the only place my cum ended up was deep in the bottom of her well.

"Go on . . . " I urged him. "Do it. Look at that dripping cunt. You know she wants it."

Slowly, Hatter positioned himself between

Alice's legs, the blunt head of his cock nudging at her entrance. Then he gently pushed the tip of his long, hard prick inside of her slick, pink orifice and eased halfway inside in one slow, smooth motion.

His eyes rolled into the back of his head before they squeezed shut. He let out a hiss as he pushed in further, savoring the tightness and warmth that now enveloped him.

Alice groaned in her sleep, drawing up one leg only to have it be gently blocked by Hatter's narrow hip. He stilled for a moment, savoring the feel of her wet heat holding him captive, before he began to move. He rocked back and forth with excruciatingly slow, deliberate thrusts, careful not to wake her.

His strokes started slow, almost lazy, but soon built to a steady rhythm. My cock was painfully hard, just aching to bury itself in her warmth and explode. I loosened my grip and started stroking myself in the same maddeningly slow rhythm as Hatter. There was something so absolutely carnal and depraved about watching my slutty little bunny be mounted and fucked by someone other than me, and all of it happening in her sleep.

Perhaps it was the knowledge that even when her mind was lost in dreams, her body was wet and ready for us at our command.

I watched, entranced, as he claimed her.

Used her.

Defiled her.

I pulled myself up to kneel beside Hatter, then licked my fingers. I reached over and began massaging her swollen pink nub while he continued to slowly glide in and out of her. The smooth skin of his cock was soaking wet with her juice, and I ached to dive into it with him, to have both our cocks stretch her wide, to give her the full force of our affection.

But we'd have to work up to that.

The longer Hatter fucked her unconscious body, the more my control frayed at the seams. The need to bury myself inside her heat and take everything I wanted was growing stronger with every stroke of Hatter's cock . . . every flex of his thighs and his ass as his wet dick slid in and out . . . in and out.

But I didn't want this to end, the raw intimacy we shared, the claiming of our sleeping beauty. Taking her like this was a balm for the emptiness I'd felt ever since Alice left our world.

Hatter gripped her hips, holding her in place as he pumped harder.

Faster.

Alice's hips twisted as she whimpered, then groaned. Then she let out a gasp as her eyes fluttered open.

For a moment, a stunned look of surprise took over her beautiful face, as if she didn't know whether to be terrified or delighted. In a burst of possessiveness, I pushed Hatter off of her and climbed on top, skewering her so deep that my balls were smashed against her ass.

And then, while I was lodged inside her, pinning her to the mattress, I transformed into my demon form.

Alice screamed as my horns crept out of my head and my black wings sprang out from my shoulders. The human cock swelled thicker and thicker, then finally split into two, stretching my bunny until she wailed from the way I made her burn.

"Make her shut up!" I told Hatter as I began to pound the narrow gash. Alice howled until she nearly choked on the fae cock being stuffed into her mouth.

Hatter grasped a handful of hair at the back of her neck with one hand, angling his body to give me a perfect view of him face-fucking Alice. I groaned as her lips closed around his wet cock, hot and wet and perfect. She sucked hard, hollowing her cheeks, and his hips bucked involuntarily.

She moaned around his cock, the vibrations racing through him, and he growled, "Just like that, Alice. Such a good girl."

Meanwhile, I rode her like she was the last fuck I'd ever enjoy in this world.

The dual sensations threatened to undo me, pleasure coiling tight in my gut.

She arched her hips upwards to try her best to accommodate my dual shafts as I plundered and pillaged her tight, wet hole. But I could tell she'd never had two in there at once. The closest she'd experienced was Chess with his monster cock.

He was big. There was no arguing with that.

But taking two different cocks in the same hole . . . that wasn't for a novice.

That skill was reserved for sluts and whores.

And for slutty little bunnies . . . like my Alice.

The scent of sex hung heavy in the air, all three of us panting in the heat of the moment. I stroked a hand down Alice's flank, feeling her quiver under my touch.

"You're behaving so well for us," I murmured, meeting her gaze. Her eyes were glazed with lust, lips swollen from taking Hatter's relentless cock. "Are you ready for your reward?"

She nodded, unable to speak.

With precise, serpentine movements, I rolled against her clit, creating heat and friction that nearly had her sobbing for release.

She jerked under me with a strangled moan, desperate for more.

"Come," I said softly. "That's it, bunny. Come for daddy. Show me how much you love having two cocks in your pussy at the same time."

Her mouth opened wider to gasp.

She was so close. So fucking close.

"Show me what a little slut you are, getting fucked in your pussy with two demon cocks while you're choking on my friend's dick."

She shattered with a wail, her inner walls clenching around my cocks in a vice-like grip as her orgasm crashed over her in waves. Her moans filled the room, her hands fisting in the sheets as she came with a scream. I watched her legs flail and slide up and down the sheets as she moaned past the hard, hot meat still battering her sweet, slutty mouth.

I began pounding into her with a primal urgency, my grunts mingling with the sound of wet flesh on flesh. Her cunt continued to tighten and tug on my shafts.

"Fuck her harder," Hatter panted, still cramming his length past Alice's soft, wet lips. "Make it so she can't walk after you're done."

I obliged, picking up the pace, her wetness coating my crotch as my climax neared. Alice cried out, her nails raking down my back, catching on my wings as I started to fuck with wild abandon. I took her hard and deep, angling to hit the exact spot that would make her come again.

I wouldn't be satisfied until I'd emptied my balls deep inside her.

"Come on, you little whore. Show me how bad you want my cum!"

Within seconds, her inner walls clenched around me as she peaked again with a feral wail. The coils of heat in my gut drew tighter, an unbearable pressure that demanded release.

I groaned, thrusting deep, claiming her as mine.

My balls drew up, and I surged forward, filling her in one final thrust, spilling myself in her warmth. Her insatiable pussy milked my seed from me, wrenching every last drop from my cock as I trembled with the force of my climax.

I opened my eyes and met Hatter's gaze. His eyes were heavy-lidded, pupils blown wide with lust as he buried himself into Alice's mouth.

A few more pumps, and I knew he was about to lose control.

"Come in her mouth," I huffed, still thrusting as I

caught my breath. Then I turned to Alice. "And don't you *dare* swallow it!"

Her muffled response was indecipherable, but I knew what she was saying.

Yes, my king.

Finally, with a soft groan, Hatter fisted his hands in Alice's hair, guiding her to take more of him. He reached his peak and used both of his hands to fuck her beautiful face. I watched in approval as his narrow hips snapped faster and faster.

He repositioned one leg to give himself more leverage, inadvertently giving me a perfect view of his balls as they slammed against her wet chin. Finally, they twitched and unleashed their contents into the back of Alice's throat.

"Don't swallow!" I repeated. My bunny obediently blinked and nodded her head as hot, pulsing ropes of semen blasted the roof of her mouth and coated her tongue. Creamy white fluid appeared at the corners of her mouth, hinting that she'd received an impressive load.

A deviant smile spread across my face. "Give it back to him."

She shot me a puzzled look as Hatter slowly inched his cock out of her mouth.

"You took something from him. Now give it back. He knows what to do."

Hatter's eyes gleamed, and a deviant grin spread across his face. He leaned forward, capturing Alice's mouth in a searing kiss as he sealed his lips to his. I watched, transfixed by the sight of their mouths melding together, and the sight of Hatter as he reached down to scoop up the cum dripping from Alice's chin. I hummed in approval as she transferred an entire mouthful of his essence back into his own, intensifying their connection.

Hatter broke the kiss and pressed his lips together, leaning back to meet my gaze. A string of cum and saliva stretched between him and Alice—a sight that sent a fresh spike of heat straight to my groin.

I slid my cocks out of her trembling form, then lifted up her hips so that her legs dangled down my back and her ass was propped up against my chest. Her pussy glistened, swollen and dripping with our combined release.

I spread her gash apart with my thumbs until her gaping cunt looked more like a wishing well. She whimpered, squirming against my powerful grip.

"Ransom, please."

"Look at her," I said hoarsely to Hatter, who made a strangled sound of agreement. "Look at our beautiful little slut."

Alice glanced up at me, her eyes dancing with both defiance and obedience, before she nodded in agreement.

I fought the urge to throw Alice down on her stomach and take her from behind, to chase the mindless pleasure that hovered just out of reach.

Instead, my gaze locked on the glistening pink folds under my nose until she yielded to the demands of my hungry stare.

A wicked grin curled my lips, and I began circling her clit with a wet finger. Anticipation and arousal coursed through me as Hatter crawled over to us and positioned his mouth above her gaping pussy.

"Well?" I prompted him. "Don't keep my bunny waiting too long."

On perfect cue, he spit his hot seed deep into her already swollen and sensitive core.

Alice groaned, arching her back as the hot liquid dripped into her hole. Hatter leaned close as the two of us watched our cum gather and pool at the bottom of her well.

"Make a wish," I told him.

"Already done, my friend," he sighed before tumbling on the bed next to Alice. "Have you made yours?"

"I have."

"Do I get to make a wish?" Alice asked.

I shook my head.

"No bunny. You're the well."

Using my demonic incubus powers of arousal, I warmed my fingers and made them vibrate and hum until Alice was writhing and bucking against me. I held her against my chest, keeping her pussy aimed at the ceiling until her inner walls trembled and swallowed up the offering she'd just received.

"Please," she whimpered again. "Hatter . . . Ransom . . . I need you guys to fuck me again!"

"Can't do that now, I'm afraid," I said with genuine disappointment. "You're the well. You're the one who grants the wishes. Let's see which one of us wins."

She gave me an adorable, endearingly frustrated frown.

Poor thing really *did* want to get fucked again.

"I don't understand."

"Get on your hands and knees, and keep your ass towards us."

Bless her . . . she did exactly as she was told.

"Yes, my king."

I'd trained her well.

Just hearing those words made me want to fuck her again. But if I did that, it would ruin the game.

"Perfect. Now stay there."

"For how long?"

Using her sheets to wipe off my dicks, I snickered and shrugged.

"As long as it takes for our cum to drip down to your knees. Whoever's seed stays inside you the longest gets their wish granted."

Alice craned her neck around and shot me a nasty glare.

It was precious.

"You guys are freaks!"

"No," Hatter began, "We're smart. If Chess were here, he'd win. He always wins the Wishing Well game."

Alice narrowed her eyes at us, but she stayed still. A thin trickle of semi-clear, opalescent cum began to seep out of her cunt and crawl down her left inner thigh.

"If he always wins, why hasn't he wished for the ability to stop losing his powers every time he comes?"

Hatter laughed softly, and we both shared a grin.

"That's an excellent question. I suppose you'll have to ask him next time you see him."

My eyes burned with raw hunger as I watched the glistening trail creep further down her her inner thigh, drawing my attention to the flushed skin and tangle of sheets beneath her.

Without hesitation, Hatter ran his forefinger through it and tasted it. The smirk playing across his lips immediately told me that I'd lost our Wishing Well game.

"Looks like I win again."

The sharp scent of sex still hung in the air, draping the room in a thick musk. It should've smelled like sweet ambrosia to me, but the surrender of my defeat had left a bittersweet taste on my tongue.

"Fine," I said with a sigh. "What's your wish?"

"To have Alice all to myself . . . while you make all of us breakfast." He caressed her ass, then pulled himself onto his knees beside her. He glanced down at her and gave her a seductive wink. "You did say you wanted to get fucked again, didn't you?"

She bit her lip and nodded. But when she caught my gaze, she let her lip fall back into place.

"I did say that," she replied, still looking straight at me. "I like pancakes. And veggie omelettes. Easy on the cheese."

That devious little brat.

But then again, she'd been locked up in a mental institution. Making her breakfast was the least I could do.

"Very well," I said, raising my hands in a rare act of surrender. "Hatter, do you have any special requests?"

"No. Just don't interrupt us. We'll come down when we're ready."

"Don't keep her up here too long," I warned as I climbed out of the bed and headed for the door. "I'm sure she's worked up quite an appetite."

I headed downstairs, trying to push away the tinge of jealousy inside me. It wasn't that Alice was getting fucked, it was that I'd lost my own game.

I might need to consider adjusting the rules.

I was debating the best way to go about it when I wandered into the kitchen and stopped dead in my tracks.

Every direction I looked, there, on every wall, every counter, every cabinet and crisscrossing over the refrigerator, were thin, slimy trails of blue.

Fear coursed through me as I recognized the unmistakable evidence of the Red Queen's spies.

I don't know how she'd done it, but Roxanne knew where Alice was.

We had to get out of here, and we had to go *now*.

CHAPTER FOUR

ALICE

I gasped as Hatter's hands gripped my hips from behind, holding me in place as he plunged into me again and again. My back arched and my ass lifted up to meet his thrusts, pleasure building with each stroke. The sweet friction of our bodies moving together was intoxicating, beckoning me closer to ecstasy.

His feverish fingers reached around and found my clit again, sending ripples of warmth through my body. The only thing hotter than dreaming about him licking my pussy and fucking me was waking up and seeing he was actually licking my pussy and fucking me.

I groaned and pushed my pussy against his warm fingers, imagining the insane grin on his face now that he finally had me all to himself.

"Don't stop," I breathed. "I'm gonna come!"

"That's it . . . come all over me, Alice."

His hands gripped my waist, pulling me closer

against him as his thrusts quickened. I was so close, teetering on the edge of another orgasm when the bedroom door burst open.

A loud bang shattered our intimate moment. The bedroom door flew open, banging against the wall. Ransom burst in, his dark eyes wild as they scanned every corner of my bedroom. He was still in his demon form.

And still totally naked.

I blinked, dazed from the interruption, heart pounding. If he was here to join us, I wasn't going to turn him away.

"This is a private party," Hatter complained as he continued fucking me. "Can't you see we're busy?"

"The Red Queen knows where we are," Ransom panted, leaning against the doorway. "Or she's about to find out very soon." The urgency in his voice cut through the haze of lust.

Fear and adrenaline raced through my veins, banishing any remnants of arousal. Hatter froze, still buried deep inside me.

"How can that be?"

Ransom shook his head, then began inspecting the room. He looked behind curtains, behind my furniture, and under the bed.

"I don't know. There are at least a dozen blue pills crawling around the house at this very moment. We have to find each one and destroy them before they reach Roxanne!"

My heart seized and my eyes widened as I realized the implication of his words. The blue pills weren't just slimy worms—they were the Red Queen's spies, programmed to seek her out her the moment they were activated. If she found me, it would mean off with my head.

Literally.

I pushed off of from Hatter's hips, disentangling our bodies, and hurried to get dressed.

Pulling on a pair of running shorts and a cropped sweatshirt, I followed my wicked boys downstairs to survey the destruction in my kitchen.

The skylights let in the bright late morning sunshine, drenching most of my main floor in crisp, clear light. That brightness made it crystal clear what was wrong.

A network of slimy cobalt-blue lines stretched across every surface of my kitchen . . . every wall in the living room . . . and the dining room. Each one seemed to lead away from the kitchen and towards a window or a door.

My stomach churned at the sight.

"I counted thirteen trails," Ransom said, and pointed to a cabinet where I kept my blender and all my supplements. All the blue lines seemed to have come out of that same cabinet. "They all originated here. Alice, do you know why that might be?"

I gripped the counter, rage burning in my chest.

"That's where Dinah kept the supplements she used for my smoothies," I told them. "There's a box of different jars and tins. I never paid attention to what was in them. I just thought it was powdered kale or some shit like that."

Yanking open the drawer next to the stove, I grabbed an oven mitt and used it to open the cabinet so I wouldn't have to touch the blue slime with my bare hands.

I immediately jumped back and started screaming.

It wasn't from seeing a jar of powdered kale.

I was screaming at the fat, blue worm the size of a cucumber clinging to the other side of the cabinet door. A small protrusion came out of the hole at the end facing me and I screamed again as a spiral of tiny spikes swirled round and round, like its mouth was a tiny drill.

Still completely buck naked in his full demon form, Ransom grabbed a saucepan from the pot and pan rack overhead, then began beating the shit out of the worm, destroying the cabinet door in the process.

I didn't care.

Not when my house was infested with slimy fat slug-worms with drill-mouths that were spying on me.

"One down. Thirteen more to go," Ransom huffed before eyeing my marble rolling pin and handing it to Hatter. He tossed his hair out of his eyes, some of it catching on one of his black horns. "Help me track them down. Focus on inspecting the doors and windows. If we don't act fast, Roxanne will know Alice's exact location within minutes."

"Where the hell is Jack?" I demanded. "We need all the help we can get!"

Hatter shrugged. "He's probably curled up in a

dark hole somewhere since he can't be out in the sunlight." His mismatched eyes drifted around my sun-drenched kitchen, falling on a blue trail that had tunneled through my patio door. "I'll start looking around the pool."

"I'll take the opposite side of the house, and we'll do a full sweep of the property," said Ransom. His fingers tightened around the handle of the saucepan. "We have to annihilate each and every one of them."

As he and Hatter prepared to leave, panic bubbled in my chest. I didn't want to be left alone. Not again.

Hatter cupped my face and kissed me, slow and deep. "Stay here. We'll be back before you know it."

"That's always the last thing they say in horror movies, and then the next thing you know, there's a murderer in the house."

"You'll be fine. Jack's around here somewhere. He won't let anything happen to you. He swore that he would protect you with his life."

The comment caught me off guard.

"He did?"

"Mmm hmm . . . " Hatter hummed while toying with my hair. "I don't know what you did to that sanctimonious fuck . . . " His genuine curiosity melted into a smirk. "Well, on second thought, I have a fairly good idea of what you did to him."

He shot me a seductive wink and started to walk away, but I caught his hand, clinging to him.

"Be careful."

Hatter squeezed my hand before letting it go, his

eyes softening at the sight of my distress. "We will. We'll take care of this and be back before you know it."

Ransom placed a quick kiss on my forehead. "We need to hurry. It shouldn't take long."

They left in a flurry of makeshift weapons and determination. I sagged against the counter, staring at the broken cabinet door and the blue mess of chunky worm guts on my kitchen floor.

Part of me wanted to cry . . . the part of me that Chess understood. I knew if he was here, he'd curl me into his chest and let me sob.

The other part of me . . . the part that had spent the last few weeks training with Jack, refused to shed a tear. I took a deep breath and steeled my nerves. There would be time to analyze all my anger and feelings of betrayal later. For now, I needed to focus on damage control.

Bile rose in my throat as I looked at the cabinet where Dinah kept her stash of "supplements" for my daily smoothies. How had I never suspected my personal assistant of doing anything remotely shady? All this time, she'd been plotting against me. Poisoning me, bit by bit.

I realized she'd been drugging me for years. *Years!* All the missing hours of my life, the foggy memories . . . I'd blamed it all on the fact that I liked to let loose and party. But the truth was that it had been Dinah manipulating me the entire time.

Anger boiled in my veins. She'd been the closest thing I'd had to a best friend for so long. But it had all been an act, a scheme to keep me weak and vulnerable. I vowed that whenever I saw her again, that bitch would pay for her betrayal. The Red Queen may have corrupted her, but Dinah was far from innocent.

No, she'd made an active choice to poison me, to drug me, every single day. The memory of Dinah's blue smoothie she had faithfully brought me every morning now turned my stomach. I had zero doubt that every single one of them had been spiked with those blue pills to keep me passive and trusting, primed for Roxanne's manipulation.

Using a long pair of barbecue tongs, I reached into the box of supplements and took out each item, setting them on the counter next to the sink for inspection.

A packet of spirulina.

A jar of protein powder.

A bottle of turmeric capsules.

Then I saw a small blue box with the lid partially out of place. Still using the tongs, I lifted the lid away and gasped at the contents.

There must've been at least fifty or sixty neon blue pills inside, all of them either squirming or actively hatching. The second I lifted the lid, they started wiggling more and more, growing faster and faster.

Oh, fuck no.

I choked back a revolted scream, trying desperately to think of how I'd manage to kill so many at once. They were so wiggly and crawling in different directions. I thought about carrying them to the pool, but I knew I wouldn't make it there fast enough to drown them.

But the water gave me an idea.

I flipped on the hot water in the sink to full blast. Then, trying as hard as I could to keep my hand steady, I grasped the box with the barbecue tongs and brought it over to the sink, tipping it gently.

One by one, the worms and the pills slid down the drain. I slammed the box against the side of the sink until I'd emptied every last blue pill. But when I glanced down, some of the bigger ones were crawling out of the drain.

Enraged and terrified, I grabbed the sprayer and rinsed them back down with the steaming hot water, then flipped on the garbage disposal.

It gurgled and churned as if I'd shoved ten pounds of jelly into it. Blue spray and tiny blue chunks splattered against the white walls and white upper cabinets. I panted in relief, knowing the worms were obliterated.

My mind was racing with anger and betrayal towards Dinah for her years of lies and manipulation.

I let out a slow breath, trying to calm my anger. Now wasn't the time to waste energy getting pissed off. There were more immediate problems to deal with, like the worm invasion that had taken over my house.

The kitchen was a disaster. Cabinets and drawers were full of holes, food containers overturned, with their contents spilled across the floor. A box of cereal had been infiltrated, leaving puffed rice scattered everywhere like mummified maggots. And everywhere, those nasty blue trails—slime tracks were leading toward every door and window of my house.

My lip curled in disgust, but I had to clean it up if I didn't want to attract more bugs. I grabbed a bunch of cleaning supplies from under the sink and started scrubbing at the blue spray, the blue chunks, and the blue slime trails, erasing every trace of blue within my reach.

I was wiping down the lower cabinets when I heard the front door swing open.

"That was fast," I called out to the guys from the floor.

No reply.

Maybe they were talking to each other. Hatter was fae, after all. Maybe they were having a telepathic conversation that they didn't want me to hear.

"Did you smash all the blue pills?"

Still no reply. But somebody was definitely in my house.

My head jerked up, pulse racing. I saw a figure carrying an armload of grocery bags that obstructed my view of her face.

I didn't need to see her face.

I knew *exactly* who it was.

"What the hell happened in here?" Dinah asked as she took in the sight of my kitchen. "It looks like a bunch of toddlers had a finger-paint fight."

The rage I'd felt towards her surged up again, hot and venomous. I rose to my feet and straightened, meeting her gaze without any of the fake sincerity she was using.

"Toddlers can't fly," I replied coolly, and pointed to the wandering trails that went up the walls and ceiling before escaping through the skylights.

"That's so crazy. Good thing the maids are coming tomorrow. I hope they bring a ladder."

I watched Dinah in utter disbelief as she walked past me and set the bags of groceries on the counter without another word. She started putting food in the fridge like this sort of thing happened all the time.

My eyes darted around, searching for something I could use to protect myself with. The knives were on the opposite end of the kitchen.

Dammit.

But I had a steel pepper mill that might work. I tossed the cleaning cloth into the sink and picked up the pepper mill as casually as I could.

There was nothing casual about standing around while holding a pepper mill.

When Dinah shut the door of the fridge and saw me standing there, holding it between our bodies, she lifted a curious brow.

"What's with the pepper mill? Did you want me to make you a salad?"

"I want you to get the fuck out of my house!" I snapped, not taking my eyes off of her for a second.

"Alice? What's wrong? Are you okay?"

"Am I *okay*?" I mocked. "Don't play innocent with me, you bitch! I know what you did! I know all about the blue pills, the magic smoothies you were drugging me with. I know all about your lies!"

Dinah's mouth dropped open in confusion. "I—I don't know what you're talking about. Have you eaten anything today? I think your blood sugar might be low."

"There's nothing wrong with my blood sugar!" I snarled, gripping the pepper mill tighter. "How long have you been working as a spy for the Red Queen and keeping me away from Wonderland?"

Her lips curved into a smug smile, and she rolled her eyes before putting away a box of cereal.

"Alice, I don't know what drugs you're on this time, but I'm not a spy. I don't work for anyone except you. I'm your friend, remember?"

"You're not my friend . . . " I hissed. My hands were trembling. "A *real* friend would have visited me in my darkest moment, locked away in that institution. A *real* friend would have helped me escape from that Hell and never looked back. A *real* friend would never betray me the way you have!"

Dinah's smile only grew more sympathetic. "Alice, there's no need to be so hostile. I didn't visit you because I didn't want any paparazzi following me. The tabloids are finally starting to shut up about your mental health crisis. You know I've always had your best interests at heart."

A bitter laugh escaped me. "My best interests? You kept me away from Wonderland since I can remember! You've been manipulating me for years with your box of blue pills! Not anymore—I shoved them all down the garbage disposal!"

Dinah's surprise melted into cool indifference. "I see. It seems your little trip to Wonderland has enlightened you after all." A cruel smirk twisted her lips. "It's a shame that nothing else you've learned will do you any good now that you're back."

Her hands began to glow and crackle with magic, gathering power around her. My own rage swelled in response, and I raised the pepper mill over my head, using all of my energy to make it transform into a sword.

No magic came to aid me.

Fuck it.

I lunged at her with a snarl, ready to bash her face in with my sorry excuse for a sword.

She flung out her hand, sending sparks of magic around me, spinning me, wrapping me like a spider encasing a moth in its web. My arms clamped down to my sides against my will. The pepper mill tumbled from my grasp and fell to the floor with a clatter.

Dinah tsked and shook her head in disappointment, keeping her arm outstretched as if holding me in place with an invisible rope.

"You should know better than to fight me, Alice. I've been around a lot longer than you have. I'm older and more powerful than anyone you know."

"Not by a long shot," a familiar voice replied.

Dinah turned around to look at where the voice had come from just as a sword met her outstretched hand, slicing clean through the skin and bone. She screamed as her hand fell to the floor with a wet thud, blood gushing from the stump of her arm.

Her shrieks filled my ears, and I recoiled at the sight of the hand bouncing over to me, fingers still twitching. The magic holding me vanished, and I collapsed against the counter, gasping for breath.

Jack kept his sword pressed against her throat. "On your knees. Now."

Dinah froze, her eyes darting between Jack and the bleeding stump at the end of her arm. I could see the calculations spinning through her mind, weighing her odds, wondering if she should risk losing the other hand.

"Jack, what are you doing?" I gasped in revulsion.

"She's fae." His tone was cold and unconcerned. "It'll grow back."

Even as he spoke, I could see the stump of Dinah's arm beginning to knit itself back together. I swallowed hard, fighting not to puke, yet I couldn't look away.

After a long moment, Dinah's shoulders slumped in defeat. Slowly, reluctantly, she lowered herself to her knees, gaze fixed on the floor.

Meanwhile, every part of Jack's body that was exposed to the sunlight streaming through the windows was starting to burn. Yet he didn't flinch. The second Dinah's knees hit the floor, Jack grabbed her by her hair and dragged her kicking and screaming into the hallway and out of the sun.

A loud shout rang out. "Alice!"

Ransom rushed into the kitchen, his chest

heaving and his saucepan dripping with blue slime. "Are you alright?"

"Yeah," I shuddered as he set aside his weapon and took me into his arms. I sagged against him, my pulse racing.

Normally I would've been terrified at a hulking naked demon with horns and wings bursting through my front door and grabbing me, but I knew better with this one. Hatter was by my side a moment later.

I met his gaze, seeing my own steely determination reflected there.

"Did you find the worms?"

His mouth twisted and he narrowed his eyes. "Not all of them. Which means Roxanne knows where you are."

"A little help here," Jack called out to us from the spare bedroom.

Ransom let go of me and stormed over to where Jack was still holding Dinah. His hands curled into fists.

"How dare you show your face here?"

"She came here to bring Alice back to the Red Queen," said Jack.

Ransom's wings folded neatly behind his back, and in a swirl of black smoke, he transformed into his human form, wearing a black suit with gold pinstripes that screamed mafia demon daddy.

And he was in no mood to fuck around.

He pinned his dark-eyed glare back onto Dinah and rested his hands on his hips. "It seems we have an interrogation to conduct."

"I'm not talking to *any* of you," Dinah rasped. "Roxanne will make you suffer for this! She'll destroy everything you hold dear. Your kingdom, your people, your precious Alice..." Her gaze slid to me, filled with hatred. "Especially Alice."

"Oh, sweetheart . . . we'll make sure you talk," Hatter said with a laugh, then swung the marble rolling pin into Dinah's stomach, making her double over and groan in pain.

"Easy, friend," Jack warned. His grip was firm, keeping Dinah restrained as she struggled against him. "We need her alive."

"She can live with a few broken ribs," Hatter said with a dark laugh. His blue eye gleamed with the promise of more violence. His free hand slid down the cool stone length of the rolling pin as he gently slapped the marble against his palm. "How many teeth do you think she needs to be able to talk?"

Dinah's composure was slipping, eyes darting between the three of us nervously.

"You all know who I work for. Let's not do anything hasty, now, Hatter. I'm sure we can come to an agreement."

"Tie her up," Ransom ordered. "I don't trust this bitch."

Hatter tossed the rolling pin onto the guest bed and conjured a length of rope from the pocket of his tattered pants. He stepped over her and grabbed her arms, binding them behind her back. A moment later, Dinah let out a muffled grunt.

"That'll hold her," Hatter said grimly. "Bastard fae magic won't get through these knots."

Ransom turned to Dinah, who was trussed up on the floor, glaring daggers at us. "Tell us the Red Queen's military plans. Now."

Dinah bared her teeth. "Why should I tell you anything?"

Jack crouched down, tracing the tip of his sword down Dinah's cheek, pressing into it, but not quite breaking the skin. "You'll talk . . . because if you don't, I'll start cutting off more than just your hand."

Dinah paled but remained defiant. "You wouldn't dare."

"Try me," Jack said softly.

Dinah remained silent.

Ransom chuckled, circling her like a predator stalking prey. "Your loyalty to Roxanne is admirable, yet foolish. Once she has what she wants, do you really believe she'll let you live? You're expendable to her." He gripped Dinah's chin, forcing her to meet his golden, glowing gaze. "But not to us. Cooperate, and I'll make your captivity...pleasurable."

"Oh, I've already been there . . . done that," she said, looking down her nose at him. I tamped down the tiny flames of jealousy that ignited at the thought of Ransom taking Dinah to bed. I knew it was all bullshit.

My mafia demon daddy crouched down in front of her, his ominous eyes glowing deep amber.

"It seems a mind invasion is in order. Let's see what's really in that twisted head of yours, shall we?"

Dinah paled but said nothing. The glare she gave him was downright venomous. Unfazed, Ransom placed two fingers to each side of her temples while a cruel smile unfurled on his lips.

After a long moment, he withdrew them with a frown and rose to his full height.

"She's resisting, but I saw enough to know what the Red Queen's plans are."

"Well?" Jack growled through his teeth. "What are they?"

"Roxanne intends to unleash the Jabberwocky against Amari's soldiers within the week, then use it to sack the castle. She won't stop until her demon has destroyed the remaining defenses of the Kingdom of Diamonds and Ice."

Dinah bared her teeth in a bloody grin. "Once the Jabberwocky is unleashed, nothing will stop it. Its fire will turn the White Queen's army to dust. It will melt through the thickest walls of ice and leave the White Queen's castle a puddle of mud. Wonderland will burn, and the Red Queen will rule over the ashes."

"What's even the point of that?" I asked, unable to stop my massive eye roll. As far as I knew, Roxanne's legendary beast was her most powerful weapon. If it was turned loose, it could decimate Amari's army.

But to rule over ashes?

It didn't makes sense.

"Why is this bitch so obsessed with destroying everything?"

Jack let out a weary sigh.

"Most likely, Roxanne would rather be the ruler of her own hellscape than serve another queen in Wonderland."

"True," Ransom agreed with a somber nod. "However . . . "

A sudden blast of bright yellow light blinded me, and I covered my burning eyes. Wind rushed around me, the air filled with crackles of electricity as every hair on my body stood on end.

"What's happening?" I shouted.

As fast as it happened, the whirlwind disappeared, leaving me to stare at Jack, Ransom, and Hatter, in search of an explanation.

My eyeballs saw it before my brain could register.

"FUCK!" Ransom bellowed before falling to his hands and knees to look under the bed.

Dinah was gone.

CHAPTER FIVE

ALICE

All that was left of Dinah was a pile of rope sitting at Jack's feet.

"I—I tied the knots tight," Hatter stammered in disbelief.

We all knew he was thinking sharper than ever, thanks to the powers of my magic pussy. Getting laid seemed to be the only thing that helped him focus.

"Her hand must've grown back faster than we realized," Jack said with a grim expression. "She was probably working at the knots from the moment you tied her up."

Ransom rose to his feet and looked me up and down.

"You can't stay here, Alice. Dinah will go straight to the Red Queen and tell her where you are. She'll send her soldiers to come for you at any moment."

"He's right," Hatter agreed. He took off his top hat and turned it round and round in his hands, carefully inspecting the brim. "It's too dangerous for you to remain here now that she knows your location. We must return to Wonderland at once."

Jack sheathed his sword and tossed his long hair over his shoulder.

"We all know you never asked for any of this, Alice. You don't have to fight Amari's war. Not if you don't want to. I'll fight in your place. I've already told Her Majesty that I'm duty-bound to protect Wonderland's people. And you . . . "

He trailed off, his red eyes unwavering. "You are my people."

"Jack . . . " My throat swelled up with big, deep emotions. I bit my lip, my heart aching at his declaration.

Wonderland had taken some getting used to, but now it felt like my second home. It felt better than this huge empty house that nobody came to visit. It felt better than the fake friends who couldn't be bothered to bust me out of the mental health facility I had been locked away in.

I cared about the people who lived in Wonderland . . . three of them were standing right in front of me.

I didn't want to die trying to save it . . .

But I couldn't let it burn to ashes.

Ransom cupped my face, reading the conflict in my eyes. "What have I told you about biting your lip, bunny?"

Before I could respond, he leaned down and nipped at my mouth, then whispered, "That's my job.

No matter if you're here, or if we're back in Wonderland."

"Can you flirt with Alice on the way back home?" Hatter said, sounding unusually impatient. "The Red Queen's soldiers are at the door."

Jack's hand was already on his sword, but he didn't draw it. Instead, he pulled me close as the sound of men kicking in my front door echoed in the front hall.

"Shit! What do we do?" I whispered. I could hear the soldiers fanning out in the kitchen. They'd find us in a matter of seconds.

Hatter pulled at the brim of his hat and stretched it into the size of a hula hoop. "Hurry along now. This thing's not nearly as reliable as the usual rabbit holes."

Jack whisked me into the giant top hat, with Ransom right behind us. I was surrounded by complete darkness and the smell of Hatter's hair. Something hard and warm bumped into me, and I smelled freshly brewed tea. Then sweet frosting of cupcakes and cherries.

A pale blue light bloomed in front of me, and I immediately recognized the crisp, ozone top notes of the air whooshing towards me.

"Almost there," Jack murmured near my ear.

"Hatter's about to close his end," Ransom huffed. "All together now, on the count of three! One . . . "

"Three!" Hatter yelled while shoving all of us into the pale blue light. The moment we stepped out of Hatter's top hat portal, I could feel the change in the atmosphere.

The air crackled and popped with energy as I landed on cold, hard stone. Jack fell on top of me, shielding me from the impact of Ransom and Hatter piling on top of us.

I thought we'd arrived in the White Queen's castle, but the scent of mud and sweat told me otherwise.

The sharp, crisp smells of wintry air had been replaced with distinctive and complex aromas. I could smell hot metal and burning coal. Smoke lingered in the air, heavy with the scent of salty, musky, masculine sweat.

Metallic clangs rang out in a lazy rhythm, nothing like the delicate wind chimes that hung from so many tents and trailers at Coachella.

Jack waited for Hatter and Ransom to crawl off of him before he rose to his full height and pulled me back onto my feet. I watched with fascination as Hatter's top hat shrank in his hands back to normal size. He put it on his head with a flourish that somehow managed to be both elegant and chaotic.

He adjusted the brim and grinned at me, seemingly unfazed by the sudden change in location. I had no idea where we were, but we were standing on a spacious covered stone balcony overlooking a vast courtyard. Judging by the guards patrolling the ramparts—who were dressed in the White Queen's signature armor—it seemed to be some kind of military fort.

They'd seen us, and done nothing.

Thank fuck.

We were safe.

Down below, small groups of armored soldiers were engaged in feats and fights that defied gravity, leaping and twirling in the air as if part of a choreographed dance. Archers were taking aim at targets that vanished and reappeared, their arrows trailing sparks of brilliant colors behind them.

The clang of metal was accompanied by the melodic chimes of enchanted weapons. The air was filled with the sounds of hearty laughter and chatter from the soldiers as they formed a circle inside the center of a massive outdoor courtyard.

"Where are we?" I asked, leaning out of a massive arched window to watch the men battle each other.

"We're in the Kingdom of Diamonds and Ice, on the grounds of Queen Amari's estate," Jack said as he joined me at the balcony, making sure to stay out of the sunlight. He pointed to the right, and I quickly recognized the tall spires of Amari's castle. "The castle is the Her Majesty's domain. The military camp belongs to me."

Ransom crossed his arms over his chest and raised a wily eyebrow.

"Is that so?"

Jack scoffed at him. "Yes. It is."

"Then why is Queen Amari down there, giving everyone orders without your blessing?"

Jack's red eyes flickered and narrowed as he

peered down at the training exercises taking place without him.

I leaned forward, taking in the scene unfolding before us.

Sure enough, Amari was down in the center of the courtyard.

She'd traded her usual stunning white dress for a set of formidable armor. Her purple curls had been tied back, but they still bounced and bobbed with each powerful stroke of her sword as she sparred with one of the soldiers.

Winston the White Rabbit observed from nearby, looking very official as he observed the training session and scribbled notes on a small pad of paper. Amari was holding her own, but I could see her exhaustion in the way her elbows kept falling, and the sluggishness of her parries.

"She's been at it for hours," a silky voice purred nearby. Slowly, Chess materialized on my other side. His brilliant green eyes were brimming with barely contained excitement as he wrapped his arms around me.

"I'm so glad you've returned." His gaze slid to Jack and a full Cheshire grin spread across his face. "And still in one piece, I see."

Jack shot him a warning look, his jaw feathering. "Of course she's in one piece. I would never let any harm befall her under my watch."

Chess's grin only widened at Jack's haughty possessiveness.

"Of course, of course," he purred, though his tone

implied he thought otherwise. His eyes roamed over me with longing, eyeing my cropped sweatshirt and running shorts with raw desire, no doubt recalling our last erotic encounter.

A flush rose to my cheeks under his intense gaze. When he dipped down to kiss me, his half-erect dick pressed into my bare thigh, and I couldn't help letting out a groan.

A groan that Jack ignored.

He was back to watching Amari practice her sword fighting down in the courtyard.

I wondered if he'd still ignore me if I leaned forward on the balcony and let Chess fuck me from behind.

"We could try it and find out," Chess hummed before nipping at my ear lobe.

I closed my eyes, feeling my nipples harden beneath his caress, feeling my sore pussy awaken at the prospect. Chess's hands ran up and down my body, skimming under my sweatshirt and toying with my nipples.

They danced their way down my ribcage and around my waist, then down my inner left thigh . . . then back up my right thigh. His warm hand cupped between my legs, stroking me . . . massaging me through the flimsy nylon fabric.

I leaned into his touch, pushing my ass against his hard cock, taunting him to pull down my running shorts and slide into my wetness. When I looked over my shoulder at him, his eyes were smoldering with a hunger that matched my own.

"I didn't know our queen was such an accomplished swordswoman," Ransom mused, yanking me out of my haze.

Another time . . . I thought.

Soon . . . Chess replied in my mind.

I cast a sideways glance at Ransom. He was leaning against the stone railing, watching as Amari parried a blow that would have left a less skilled opponent reeling.

His dark eyes were shadowed with concern as he watched Amari stumble back a step, nearly tripping over her own feet.

"Ever since you left, she's thrown herself into her training," Chess told him. "Always pushing herself to be better. As if she plans to fight the Jabberwocky herself."

I winced as one of the soldiers landed a blow against Amari's side. She grunted in pain but kept her guard up, circling around for another attack.

Suddenly she tripped, falling to one knee. Her opponent hesitated, uncertainty flickering across their face. With a snarl, Amari launched herself at them, her sword flashing in a flurry of blows that sent them stumbling back.

"Damn it!" she shouted, frustration evident in her voice. "Don't hold back just because I'm your queen! If I'm going to face my sister, I need to be prepared for *anything*!"

Ransom turned to Jack with concern.

"Tell your soldiers to stop this. She'll wear herself into the ground at this rate."

Jack gave him a skeptical look. "You think fighting in battle will be any easier?"

Ransom's mouth pressed into a flat line, and it was obvious that Jack had made his point. It didn't stop him from proving it further. "Amari is as stubborn as she is kindhearted. That's why Winston's down there, making observations of every weakness she has. She knows she can learn from her failures . . . that it'll make her stronger."

His voice was low and filled with admiration, and I could see why. There was something undeniably captivating about watching Amari fight; it was as if each swing of her sword was an extension of her very soul, a dance of passion and determination that left me breathless.

A dry, rasping cough drew my attention to the shadows. Whirling around, I saw a thin, elderly man shuffling forward into the light, his movements slow and unsteady. I blinked at the sight of him, struck speechless when I saw him take a drag of a cigarette and cough out a cloud of orange smoke.

"Callister..." I whispered, my voice filled with concern. "What happened to you?"

He didn't just look old . . . he looked *ancient*. Deep lines were now etched into his face and neck. His beautiful tattoos of snakes and insects were blurry and faded, warped by sagging, wrinkled skin.

His bright teal pompadour was now a thinning, pastel mess of pale green dragged over his spotted scalp. His once-brooding, magnetic eyes seemed dull, as though the weight of his advanced years was crushing him beneath their heavy burden.

How was that possible?

Only days had passed since I last saw him.

My heart twisted at the sight of him. What else had I missed in my absence? How was it that Amari was a warrior and Callister was on death's door?

What other changes had swept through Wonderland while I was gone?

Guilt rose in my throat, bitter as day-old burnt coffee. I'd abandoned them. My family, my people—I'd turned my back on Wonderland in its hour of need.

Callister wheezed, peering up at me with droopy, watery eyes. "Alice," he rasped. "You've come back."

I swallowed against the burning in my eyes and throat.

"What the hell happened to you, Callister? I was only gone for a few days!"

"Time works differently in Wonderland," he mumbled, not bothering to take the cigarette out of his mouth.

"I'm sorry," I whispered, and carefully hugged his brittle body. "I'm so, so sorry. I had no idea."

He gave a sarcastic little laugh and shook his head, offering me a shaky smile. "You're here now. That's all that matters."

If only it were that simple.

But for now, I returned his smile and blinked back my tears.

"I don't understand," I said, turning to Chess for answers. "How long was I gone?"

He chuckled, his eyes gleaming with mischief. "Not very long at all . . . although at times, it felt like forever."

"I'm worried about Callister. Nobody's supposed to get that old that fast," I protested, incredulous at the lack of concern about his friend. Nobody—not Jack, not Ransom, not even Hatter seemed to give two shits that Callister looked like he had one foot in the grave. "This is *not* normal. Why isn't anybody doing anything? Isn't Amari a doctor or healer or whatever?"

As if to prove my point, Callister coughed, his voice weak and ragged. Chess merely shrugged, unable to tear his gaze away from the courtyard below.

"It's nothing. Just the passage of time. Shifters like Callister age differently from humans and demons. Oh!" He gestured towards the training session. "Did you see that blow Amari just landed?"

I leaned over the balcony, but I was too late. All I saw was a soldier lying on his back for a moment before another one reached out to help him up.

"That's enough!" Amari's command cut through the air, her voice carrying up to us on the wind. She stumbled back, chest heaving with exertion as she searched for breath.

As if on cue, the courtyard fell silent. Her soldiers gathered around her like a pack of loyal wolves around their alpha female. They stood at attention, some of them wiping sweat from their brows, their curious gazes all turned towards their queen.

Amari stood in the center of them all, dirt smeared across her cheek and a determined set to her jaw. She scanned the faces of her soldiers, resolve and regret warring in her pale eyes.

When she finally spoke, her voice rang clear as a bell over the courtyard.

"Listen to me. What I'm about to tell you is not an easy thing. I have wronged you all."

Murmurs rippled through the crowd. Despite her somber expression, Amari lifted her chin and forged on.

"I have wronged not only you, my devoted army, but also every citizen of the Kingdom of Diamonds and Ice. Truth be told, I have wronged every single living creature in all of Wonderland. I have made mistakes. Grave mistakes. Now I have the audacity to come to you with my confessions and ask for your forgiveness."

"Confessions?" some of the soldiers murmured. "What could she possibly have to confess?"

I leaned in closer, my heart pounding as I prepared myself for whatever revelation she was about to say next. Jack mirrored my stance, his eyes narrowed in concentration.

"Many of you may have heard the recent rumors, so I'm going to set the record straight." Amari paused, swallowing hard. The vulnerability in her actions struck me, a stark contrast to the fierce warrior I'd just witnessed.

"When I was younger, I always knew my sister would use her magic for evil, so I took drastic measures to limit her abilities. I did everything within my ability to become more powerful than her. I even went so far as to . . . that is to say I . . . "

Her words trailed off, and she glanced up at the sky before doubling down and facing her troops. "I stole the Heart of Wonderland. And then I broke it."

Gasps echoed through the crowd, shock rippling across the faces of her soldiers. It was as if they couldn't believe what they were hearing.

"Talk about a turn of events," Chess remarked, amusement dancing in his eyes.

"No shit." I couldn't tear my gaze away from the scene unfolding below. "I can't believe she just outed herself to her entire army!"

Despite the weight of her words, there was a determination in Amari's eyes that demanded attention.

"Furthermore," she continued, her voice laced with remorse, "I made the desperate decision to rely on the magic of Alices from Earth to defeat Roxanne and the Jabberwocky. It was naive of me to think that these innocent girls from another realm could save us all from a problem that was caused by the imbalance between me and my sister."

"Can you believe this?" I hissed, my eyebrows raised in disbelief. "She's actually owning up to all of her bullshit!"

"Shh," Jack replied softly, not wanting to miss a single word.

The soldiers, still reeling from the initial confession, listened intently. Even from our vantage point high above, I could see that their emotions were a whirlwind of shock and loyalty.

Just like mine.

"From this moment on, I vow to face my sister the Red Queen with every last drop of my remaining strength and magic. I will no longer rely on others to fight my battles for me."

Amari's voice was unwavering, her determination palpable.

"I ask for your forgiveness and support as we stand together against our common enemy."

I held my breath, watching as her plea for forgiveness resonated with her army. Some of them looked grim . . . disappointed.

Almost despondent.

But others nodded their heads in sympathy.

In understanding.

"Will you forgive me?" She asked, her voice cracking under the weight of her shame and the vulnerability of her public confession. "Will you stand by me as we face the darkness together?"

"Of course, Your Majesty," one soldier replied, his voice full of conviction. "We are with you until the end."

"Always," another added, her eyes shining with tears of gratitude and admiration.

Amari drew her sword, the blade hissing as it slid from its sheath. Raising the sword high, she turned in a slow circle, facing all of her soldiers.

"Who else will stand with me? Who else will fight for the fate of Wonderland, as you always have? Who else will fight with me to defend our home, and our freedom?"

For a moment, Amari's plea was met by only a few murmurs. Then a soldier stepped forward, unsheathing his own blade. "I stand with you, my queen," he said, voice rough with emotion. "Always."

Another soldier moved to stand beside him. "As do I."

"And I."

A few more voices added to the mix, but it wasn't the Hollywood moment of rousing the troops that I was expecting. I knew that they were likely still processing the sheer weight of Amari's past actions, while I'd had plenty of time to mull them over.

If I'd had a sister as shitty as Roxanne, I probably would've done just about anything to stop her.

Even if it meant doing something as drastic as stealing the Heart of Wonderland.

"I stand with you, Queen Amari!" I yelled from the balcony at the top of my lungs. I waved like a maniac until she turned to face the balcony and her gaze found mine. Her eyes lit up in surprise, and for a moment, she looked like the Amari I remembered—the queen who always did the right thing. The queen who fought for justice and led with compassion.

Her lips curved into a smile, bright and brilliant as the dawn. She raised her sword, piercing the sky above her.

"And I stand with you, Alice!"

The entire courtyard erupted into cheers at the sight of me. The soldiers brandished their swords and began shouting Amari's name . . .

And *my* name.

"Long live the queen! Long live Alice!"

The cry rose, echoing from every corner of the courtyard as the soldiers rallied around Amari.

Joy and hope swelled in my chest, chasing away the shadows that had lingered there ever since I'd left Wonderland.

"Looks like you've got some competition for most beloved leader around here," Hatter teased, nudging my arm playfully.

"Nah," I replied with a small smile, watching as Amari basked in the adoration of her people. "I'll never be a queen. But if I was, I hope I'd be as good as Amari."

CHAPTER SIX

ALICE

"I'll meet you downstairs," Chess said to me and the others. His body began to disappear right in front of me. The last thing to go was his green eyes.

Hatter took off for the nearest staircase, taking two steps at a time. Ransom hoisted Callister onto his back and followed him.

I turned to Jack, now that we were alone. He was standing at the edge of shadow and light, watching me with the softest of smiles.

I shot him a flirtatious grin. "What's that look for?"

Still smiling, his gaze turned tender.

"You've made me very proud, Alice. Exceptionally proud."

"I have?" For a moment, I thought I'd heard him wrong. I'd made the White Knight proud?

"Yes," he nodded. "You displayed a skill that I cannot teach a leader. They're either born with it . . . or they're not."

I raised an eyebrow and left the balcony, stepping into the shadows where Jack stood.

"Oh really? So whatever it is, you think I was born with it?"

Jack nodded again, never taking his blood-red gaze off of me.

"I do. It's easy to stand alongside someone who is winning. Someone who is victorious. It's difficult to stand beside them when they have faltered. Your loyalty to Wonderland has not gone unnoticed."

I tilted my chin up to look at his gorgeous face.

"Is that all you noticed, was my loyalty to Wonderland?"

His soft smile faded.

"I noticed your loyalty to the people who live here," he said, reaching out to caress my cheek. I closed my eyes, nuzzling into the cool palm of his hand.

"People like you," I whispered. "I'm loyal to you, Jack."

His hand shifted at my words, and I knew I'd hit a nerve by saying them. I opened my eyes and saw his brows drawn together and jaw clenched.

"Alice..." he started, then trailed off with a sigh. His hand dropped from my face.

My heart sank.

I thought we'd been growing closer, that there was a real connection between us. Had I completely misread the signs?

"What is it?" I asked, trying not to sound as crestfallen as I felt.

He ran a hand through his white hair, looking torn. Conflicted. "It's complicated."

I folded my arms across my chest. "Then uncomplicate it. Explain like I'm five."

His red eyes met mine, an intensity in them that made my breath catch.

I saw desire.

Longing.

Hunger.

"I am loyal to you as well, Alice. More than you know."

"Why is that so complicated?" I pressed.

Jack studied me for a long moment, as if searching my face for any hint of doubt. Finding none, he slid his hand to the nape of my neck, tangling his fingers in my hair as he drew me closer. Our bodies pressed together in the shadows, and I could feel the hard lines of muscle beneath his clothes.

"Alice..." My name was a heated breath against my lips. "I serve Amari out of duty, however, I serve you out of something more. As far as I'm concerned, *you* are my queen."

"Ohhh . . . "

I couldn't deny the heat pooling between my thighs at his words. Jack was normally so reserved and closed off, to see him so vulnerable and open with me . . . was intoxicating.

Empowering.

I wanted more.

And he gave it.

"I've tried to resist you, and I have failed. I've tried to ignore the last bit of me that is human, yet I cannot. Whatever I have left of a heart . . . it's yours."

His mouth claimed mine in a searing kiss that stole the air from my lungs. It was like kissing fire itself, dangerous and addictive. Our tongues tangled together as the kiss grew more urgent, more primal.

Jack backed me against the stone wall, his body a solid weight pinning me in place. I could feel his arousal pressed against my belly, hard and insistent. He lifted my thighs, then yanked aside one of the leg openings of my shorts to force his cock inside me. I surrendered to the heat that filled and stretched me with a soft cry, lifting my hips and inviting him to sink deeper.

"I love you, Jack," I moaned against his lips, the words catching in my throat. He growled low in his chest, the sound turning me on even more. "I've wanted you since the moment we met."

"I know," he said before nipping my jawline. "I don't care if it's wrong for me to feel this way for an apprentice . . . to love you the way I do. I've imagined telling you a thousand times. But then you left."

My heart swelled at his words and I wrapped my arms around him tighter. Thanks to our blood bond, I could feel the strength of his emotions pouring into me. I knew if he was near, I'd always be safe. His hands roamed my body, making it feel like this was our first time together.

Then his tongue was on my neck, hot and wet. I sucked in a breath as his fangs pushed into my skin.

He fucked hard and fast while sucking soft and slow, and I couldn't get enough.

I was so lost in the pleasure that I didn't notice we were being watched until Jack lifted his mouth off my neck and abruptly stopped fucking me. His eyes flicked over to the stairwell, the fire inside them burning hotter than ever.

With his vampire cock still buried in me, he bared his fangs at the intruder and let out a warning growl.

"I should've known what was taking you so long," said Ransom, his deep, seductive voice breaking through the haze enveloping me. Even though Jack looked like he was about to murder the incubus, Ransom's eyes were dark with desire.
"Please . . . don't stop on my account."

Jack pulled out most of his cock, only leaving the tip in place while he licked the blood from his lips. The look in his eyes was wild . . . feral . . . completely unhinged . . .

Even though I thought I was safe in his arms, I wasn't so sure about Ransom.

That sense of danger turned me on even more, and my pussy tightened in response.

Jack's nostrils flared at the sensation. Suddenly he pulled me down onto his cock while thrusting the full length into me. I let out a cry from the force of him hitting my bruised and battered cervix. The sound would've filled the room if his hand wasn't already clamped down on my mouth.

Even Ransom winced in a mix of pleasure and pain.

"Fuck . . . you are ruthless," he hummed with half-lidded eyes. "Do that again."

"I don't take orders," Jack snarled in warning. "I *give* them!"

Ransom batted his lashes in mock innocence.

"Your queen has requested your presence downstairs. What would you like me to do, Supreme Commander? Shall I inform Her Majesty that you're too busy fucking and sucking our latest Alice to take a meeting?"

Every muscle in Jack's inhuman body was tensed up, ready to pounce. It felt like I was being held hostage by a deadly white lion—the epitome of primal masculinity, all muscle, teeth and claws, topped with a gorgeous full mane.

I couldn't help but feel a mix of pleasure and fear coursing through my body.

And I fucking *loved* it.

"You can make sure no one else comes up those stairs," Jack replied with a tone of barely restrained fury. He withdrew his cock and sank into me again, making me groan into his cool palm, which was still covering my mouth. "And if you lay a hand on Alice while I'm fucking her . . . I will rip out your motherfucking throat."

As Jack's relentless thrusting fell into a steady rhythm, Ransom made his choice. He moved from the doorway, coming closer until he was almost within arm's reach.

I could feel the heat rising in my cheeks as I watched Jack struggle with his need to possess me as his own in that moment, and his longing to give in to his own secret desires and inhibitions . . . whatever they were. In that moment, I knew that we were all caught up in a dangerous game that we couldn't escape from.

"Surely you won't mind if I get rid of those," Ransom said. With a gentle, non-threatening motion of his hand, my running shorts disappeared from my body, then reappeared in his hand. "See? I didn't have to touch her to do that."

Jack narrowed his eyes but said nothing.

"It feels better," I murmured beneath his hand. He took it away and used it to support my ass as he continued to burrow into my core. Then his mouth drifted down to my neck, his sharp teeth finding the wound from earlier.

The feel of him latching on and drinking me was better than any drug, better than any drink. The rush it gave me was almost better than sex. I couldn't help but feel one surge of adrenaline after another at the reality that Ransom was watching us, studying us, in this intimate moment.

He leaned down and angled his head to one side, watching the vampire cock that was pistoning in and out of me. Then he nodded in approval before meeting my gaze.

"That's my good little bunny, taking every inch of Jack in your tight, wet pussy. Can you feel how hard he is for you?"

"Yes," I moaned.

"You're so wet for him . . . I wish you could see how slick his cock is with your juices." Ransom gave a wicked grin, his deep voice resonating in the heavy air. "Your cunt is such a beautiful mess. Drenched in pleasure, always aching for more. You love this, don't you?"

"Yeah . . . I do."

He rose to his feet, then brought my running shorts to his nose and inhaled deeply.

"Don't drink too much now, Jack. Amari wants to meet with Alice as well. She won't be much use to anyone if she's unconscious from blood loss."

I felt the vibrations of a growl along my skin and in my veins. Jack had heard him . . . and he didn't care.

The Supreme Commander of the army of the Kingdom of Diamonds and Ice didn't take orders from anyone except his queen.

And right now, he was busy fucking her.

That's right . . . he said in my mind. *You are my queen now. Mine to serve . . .*

Ransom slinked closer to me, his seductive grin widening as he watched Jack's hips snap against mine. He let out a low chuckle, his voice a dark, sinful sound.

"Look at him, Alice. Look at how the White Knight is so utterly lost in you. Do you feel how much he wants you? How much we *all* want you?" Ransom's words were a mix of admiration and desire.

His warm breath danced against my ear and my neck, adding another layer of sensation.

Tension coiled in my belly, every spoken word having the same effect on my clit as a warm tongue swirling around it.

"Fuck . . . I feel it," I panted.

Ransom's eyes gleamed as he took another step closer. His mouth was so close to my ear that I could hear the sound of him breathing.

"Look at yourself, Alice. Look at how you're panting . . . how you're squirming. Are you sure your pussy can handle the act of being pounded by Jack's relentless cock?"

I arched my back and let out a throaty moan, eager to play along with Ransom's dirty talk. " Yeah . . . I can handle it," I gasped between Jack's powerful thrusts. "I love it when . . . when he's so deep inside me. Are you . . . are you jealous?"

"A little bit," Ransom admitted. He took another deep whiff of my damp running shorts. Then his voice dropped to a husky whisper, his words spiced with desire. "Why don't you make it better by coming for us. Be a good girl and come all over Jack's hard, slippery cock. Make him feel every pulse of your cunt as it squeezes him . . . pulls him into your heat . . . milks him until he's bone dry."

I closed my eyes and savored the sensation of being taken so roughly, so ruthlessly, up against that hard stone wall. I let Ransom's words set me on fire, matching the burn of the vampire dick that was stretching me wide.

Jack started to grind against me with a speed and intensity that had my head spinning. I could feel every inch of him, hard and hot and wet as he slid in and out. My hips arched up to meet his thrusts, to angle my clit against the heat and friction he delivered.

He withdrew his teeth and licked at my neck, then stared deep into my eyes. A storm of infinite red clouds was all I could see.

"You're so tight around him, Alice. He's losing his mind . . . can't you tell? You're driving him mad. All he wants is to come inside you, but not until you come first."

Ransom's words to me were a sinful promise. His voice purred in my ear, a sinful symphony of lust and desire, egging me on, pushing me closer to the edge.

And all the while, Jack's face was the only thing I saw. His breath hitched, and his eyes widened, pupils blown with arousal.

At that exact moment, my wave of pleasure crested, rolling through me with such intensity that my body bowed and quivered in its wake. My lungs drew in ragged breaths, each one a sharp intake as I rode the shockwaves of my orgasm.

"Yesssss . . . " Ransom groaned beside me. "Can you feel him drenching your cunt with his vampire seed? He's warm now, isn't he? So warm. Go on, Alice. Feel your pussy tug every drop out of him."

Blinking open heavy lids, I found Jack's eyes on me. Desire and reverence swirled within their crimson depths, his gaze unwavering as his cock throbbed and pulsed and unleashed liquid fire into my molten core. Our bodies melted into each other, brought there by raw desire.

He watched me with an admiration that bordered on reverence. A flush of pride washed over me at the realization of how deeply I'd affected him.

Leaning forward, Jack rested his forehead on mine, gasping as I squeezed my pussy again and again, trying to wring every drop out of him and into me.

Ransom slipped one hand into his pocket while casually twirling my running shorts around one of his fingers.

"Do you know that's the very first time Jack's ever let me watch him fuck?" He lifted a brow and looked at the White Knight, who was recovering from what could only be a mind-bending orgasm.

"Don't get used to it," Jack panted softly before gently setting me down on the ground.

"Why not? You have excellent technique. I might even learn a thing or two. That's how good you are."

Jack shot him a stern look as he tucked his dick in his pants, fastened them, and smoothed his long hair into place.

"Why are you still here, incubus? Surely that was enough to feed your demon for the next week."

Ransom shrugged in a way that made me think he was confused.

"I'm curious why you didn't keep drinking Alice's blood while you both climaxed. Seems like the sort of thing that would really get a bloodsucker off."

Jack's eyes darkened, and he ran his tongue along his lips.

"It's not worth the risk." He bit the tip of his finger and used the blood to heal the vampire bite he'd left on my neck.

"What risk?" I snatched my shorts from Ransom's finger and used them to wipe away the first dribbles of cum.

"The risk of hurting you," Jack replied.

I snorted a laugh. "I'm already hurt. I think my pussy needs a break after what you just did to me."

"That's not what I meant."

"Do tell what you actually meant," Ransom crooned with sincere interest. "It's the bloodlust, isn't it? You're afraid of completely losing control and draining all of Alice's blood, aren't you?"

Jack said nothing.

Meanwhile, I gave my shorts a firm shake, imagining that they were now clean. If my magic was working now that I was in Wonderland, this would be a great time for it to kick in.

It worked.

"Oh, hell yeah!"

"I knew it!" Ransom smirked.

"That's not it," Jack said, his tone sharp. But Ransom ignored his obvious lack of interest in discussing the topic.

"Jack, I can help you with this problem. Sexual pleasure in all its many forms is my specialty. If you'd like to experience a climax while simultaneously fucking Alice and drinking from her, the others and I can make arrangements to—"

"No."

"I'm sure if precautions were taken, Alice wouldn't—"

"I said *no*!"

Ransom threw his hands up in surrender.

"Fine, fine. But the offer is on the table, if Alice is willing."

"*I'm* not willing," Jack said with a hard stare. "It was a mistake to let you stay and watch us."

He turned on his heel and stormed down the staircase, leaving me alone with Ransom.

"You really pissed him off," I said while stepping into my clean running shorts.

Ransom shook his head.

"He's not angry at me. He's angry at himself."

I quirked a curious brow at him.

"How do you figure? He seemed pretty annoyed with you."

Showing guilt or remorse didn't seem to be an option for Ransom. The best he could do was an arrogant, smug expression.

"He's angry at himself because he knows I'm right. He doesn't want to admit it, but the truth is that Jack would love nothing more than the chance to drink your blood while coming inside of you. Letting me stay and watch him fuck you was the first step."

"I distinctly remember him saying that was a mistake," I pointed out.

A crafty smile spread across Ransom's face.

"The White Knight is the deadliest swordsman in all of Wonderland. If he didn't want me to stay and watch, he would've done something about it. Lucky for him that I enjoy the challenge of unlocking new kinks."

Filled with intrigue, I gazed up at Ransom and grinned.

"Maybe it'll be lucky for us all."

He gave me wink.

"Maybe it will."

CHAPTER SEVEN

ALICE

Ransom slipped an arm around my shoulders and guided me downstairs, where I was met with a completely different ambiance than the opulent setting of Amari's luxurious castle.

Everything here was stripped down to the bare necessities. Crystal and diamonds and intricate stained glass had no purpose here—only sturdy wood and impenetrable stone. The windowpanes were filled with dark amber glass behind iron bars, bathing the walls in rich, warm light.

Countless rows of torches lit up tapestries that hung on the walls. Each of them was embroidered with different fantastical animals or symbols, each of them speaking of a history steeped in both bravery and madness.

The soldiers, their eyes harboring stories of unseen horrors, watched me with a mix of curiosity, skepticism, and hope. Their presence served as a stark reminder that this was no ordinary training camp, but a fortress forged in the fires of Wonderland's darkest, coldest corners.

I waved weakly at a few of them before Ransom ushered me through a heavy set of wooden doors and into a huge room. The second we entered, I was struck by the sheer magnitude of the space.

The walls were lined with breathtaking paintings depicting battles from Wonderland's history, and iron chandeliers hung from the high cathedral ceilings. At the center of the room, Jack, Amari, Winston, Chess, Hatter and Callister were all standing around the biggest table I'd ever seen.

It was covered with a giant, intricately painted map. Rivers and lakes separated forests and villages. Sitting on top of the giant map were figurines of soldiers, a red castle, and a white castle that was a perfect replica of Amari's home just outside the military fort.

Despite my huge collection of worldly experiences, I couldn't shake the feeling that I was woefully unprepared for whatever was about to happen.

Amari left her spot at the table and rushed over to me, tears welling in her eyes. She immediately pulled me into a fierce hug.

"Alice! You came back!"

She let go of me, still smiling. "It's so wonderful to see you again, my dear friend."

Heat rose in my cheeks at hearing her call me a dear friend . . . especially after I'd bailed the minute things got complicated. "I'm sorry for leaving the way I did."

She shook her head, dismissing my apology, and cupped my face. "Don't be sorry, Alice. It makes sense why you didn't want to fight for someone who wasn't planning to join you in battle. You were protecting yourself."

Winston came over with two glasses of water for us, and I immediately chugged half of mine in one giant gulp.

"You gave me the wakeup call I've needed for much too long," Amari continued. "You inspired me to shed light on my past . . . on the truth. You made me want to be stronger and braver for our kingdom. Things cannot continue as they always have. You helped me realize the need for things to change."

I blinked at her, stunned.

"Oh . . . in that case, I'm glad I could help. I'm completely blown away that you had the guts to admit such a huge mistake in front of everyone. I don't think I could ever be that brave." A vision came into my mind of standing in front of that sea of soldiers, judgment etched into every one of their faces. My stomach twisted into knots.

She reached out and touched my arm gently.

"Sometimes it's easier to show courage with a sword or with magic than it is to show courage by admitting when we've made a terrible mistake. It wasn't easy to admit my mistakes to my army. But if I am to be the leader they need, I must own my faults and strive to do better. True bravery lies not only in our actions on the battlefield, but in confronting our shortcomings and working to better ourselves."

We locked eyes, and I knew she truly understood the complexity of emotions that had driven me away, and somehow, simultaneously brought me back to this world. A surge of admiration for her courage filled me, and I knew I could count on her to be a friend.

In that moment, I felt more connected to Amari than ever before. And although the world around us teetered on the brink of chaos, I knew we would face it together, bound by our shared determination to save Wonderland.

"I won't run away again, I promise."

Amari took a sip of water and motioned for me to follow her. "You came back, and that is what matters. Together, we will defeat the Red Queen and restore peace to Wonderland." She led me past Winston and all of my wicked boys to an empty chair on her left.

"Now, shall we begin planning our next move against my sister and her army?"

I nodded, waiting for her to sit down before I sank into my chair. "Hell yeah."

"Yes, it's time to end this war once and for all," Winston agreed.

I set down my glass and studied the figurines marking the positions of Roxanne's forces. Each piece was crafted with impressive detail; terrifying soldiers, grotesque creatures, and twisted landscapes leered menacingly at us, serving as a constant reminder of what we faced.

The situation looked grim, her army having advanced further into Amari's kingdom than I'd realized. The stakes were higher than ever, and my heart raced with a blend of fear and anticipation.

Jack prowled around the table, everything about him commanding us to listen as he explained the situation we were facing. Remembering the intensity of our training sessions, and how demanding he was, I couldn't help but feel a shiver of desire at the sight of him in his element.

"The Red Queen has overrun the Outer Reaches and laid siege to the Whispering Woods. There are signs of recent troop movements here. Large numbers, well-armed and armored."

He leaned past me, using a long wooden pointer to orient us to the right location. "If she takes that forest, her troops will have access to the Crossroads, and from there they can move on the castle. "

"They've been burning villages in their wake as well," Winston added. His face was grim as he surveyed the desolate landscape. "They leave nothing but ash and corpses behind."

Hatter frowned, fiddling with the brim of his hat. "Obviously, we must stop her before she reaches the forest. But with her superior numbers, a direct assault would be mad."

"Yes, it would. Which is why we need to outmaneuver her before she gets that far," Jack said, tracing a path along one of the maps. "We need to take drastic measures soon or there'll be nothing left to defend."

The chill in the air bit at my skin, highlighting the

dire situation we were in. Jack's voice cut through the tense atmosphere like a knife.

"I propose we find a way to lure the majority of the Red Queen's forces away from the woods so we can launch a surprise attack on the rest. If we can divide and conquer them, it will weaken her army enough for us to do some real damage."

"A sound strategy." Amari looked to the others for input. "My hope is for us to formulate a plan that utilizes our strengths while avoiding any direct confrontation until absolutely necessary. Does anyone have any suggestions on how to divide the Red Army?"

"We are outnumbered," said Callister. "Stealth and subterfuge will serve us far better than force alone."

Ransom leaned against the wall, arms crossed over his broad chest as his gaze slid from the maps to me. A shiver ran down my spine at the heat in his eyes, and I swallowed hard, tearing my attention away to focus on the discussion. Now was not the time for distractions, no matter how tempting.

"We could set a trap," he suggested. "Lure them into it by using Alice as the bait."

"What the fuck!" I spluttered, almost spitting out my water. "I'm not bait!"

Ransom let out a low laugh, and everyone at the table shared glances, while carefully avoiding looking at me.

Even Jack looked like he was seriously considering the idea. His red eyes were gleaming with bloodlust.

"Au contraire . . . you would be the perfect temptation to draw the Red Army out of hiding. Whatever the plan consists of, you would be safe. You have my word."

"I'd *better* have your word," I mumbled into my glass, watching it refill with water the moment I set it down. I wished it was a vodka tonic. I needed a drink after hearing this plan.

Suddenly a handful of ice cubes and a wedge of lime appeared in my glass, surrounded by what could only be tonic bubbles. I took a sip and was thrilled to discover it was the best vodka tonic I'd ever had.

"Both plans have merit." Amari rubbed her chin in thought. "Perhaps we should combine them. Create a diversion to draw part of my sister's army away, then lead the remainder into a trap to defeat them. That should weaken Roxanne enough for us to defeat her."

As the group began to debate various strategies, drawing on their unique abilities and experiences, I felt myself becoming more and more entrenched in this world—a world filled with darkness, danger, and undeniable allure. But despite the trepidation that accompanied it, I knew I was exactly where I needed to be, ready to fight for Wonderland and those I had come to cherish.

Ransom cleared his throat, drawing our attention. "Before we proceed, there is another matter we must discuss." His gaze flicked to me, a frown tugging at his lips. "I have information about the Jabberwocky."

Amari leaned forward in her chair, her brow furrowed in concern. "What of it?"

"When we were in the human world to rescue Alice, we had an encounter with Dinah."

Just hearing her name made me feel distinctly uncomfortable.

"I was able to penetrate her mind and read her thoughts. I learned that Roxanne is planning to use the Jabberwocky against our army within the week. After that, she'll have it destroy your castle. Her plan is to destroy everything within the Kingdom of Diamonds and Ice. But Dinah accidentally told me more information than she ever intended to reveal."

We all watched as his mouth curled into a wicked grin.

"She accidentally told me that Roxanne has been abusing the Jabberwocky. Torturing it to ensure its obedience and compliance in her evil commands . . . forcing it to bend to her every twisted whim. The beast has become unstable. Roxanne has been experimenting on it for years. Now it's grown savage and uncontrollable."

"Hasn't the Jabberwocky always been savage and uncontrollable?" Winston asked with a nervous twitch.

Ransom shook his head.

"It's worse now than it's ever been. Roxanne has to keep it heavily sedated to prevent it from turning on her own forces. The situation is dire, and it raises the stakes even higher for us."

"It could also be a weakness we can exploit," Jack mused. His eyes gleamed at the thought.

I rolled my eyes, my skepticism bubbling to the surface. "Seriously? You're concerned that Roxanne's demon is being abused? She created it, didn't she? Why should we care what she does to it?"

Ransom's eyes narrowed. "She didn't create it. She summoned the Jabberwocky to do her bidding. And I'll remind you that demons *do* feel pain, Alice, no matter their outward form. I'm a demon. Chess is a demon. You've seen us both experience pain."

His words resonated within me, and I remembered the way he'd saved us all from the attack at the Rabbit Hole. He'd used his demon wings to shield me from the poisoned arrows of the Red Queen's soldiers . . . and nearly lost them in the process.

"I'm sorry for not realizing that . . . I'm still getting used to how things work here," I admitted.

"You're learning quickly though, and that's what matters," Amari said with a reassuring smile before turning back to give Ransom her attention.

"The Jabberwocky might not want to carry out Roxanne's evil deeds if it's being tormented so badly by her that it's being kept sedated," he went on. "If we can learn what kind of spell it's under, we might be able to free it from Roxanne's control."

"Removing the Jabberwocky from the Red Queen's forces would be instrumental in our victory over her," Jack pointed out. "We have no match of its equal."

"I don't know that kind of spell it would be controlled by," Amari said with a frown. "I'd have to search through my spell books and see if I have any guides for how to control a demon. It might take some time."

"We don't have much time," Callister croaked from the other end of the huge table. "Not if the Red Queen is planning to attack within the next week. Her army far outnumbers our own. I say we gather more intelligence. We have to work smarter, not harder."

"We could launch a surprise attack." Hatter drummed his fingers on the table, his brows drawn in thought. "Catch them off guard before they have a chance to dig in."

Amari shook her head. "Roxanne would see that coming. She'll have safeguards in place."

"Then we target those safeguards first," said Winston. "Sabotage her supply lines, weaponry, and modes of transport. Slow her down and pick off her forces in the resulting chaos."

"It's too risky. She'll be expecting something obvious like that." Chess pointed out. "We should fortify our borders instead. Set traps, use the terrain to our advantage. Let Roxanne come to us so we can defeat her on our own terms."

"We don't have enough soldiers to fight her army and fortify our borders," Jack explained. "I can't have our troops stretched so thin. It will leave us vulnerable to attack."

"Then we need to be two steps ahead of her at all times," Chess replied before brushing a piece of lint from his tuxedo. "I can use my powers of invisibility to move among the soldiers and eavesdrop on their plans. I've already discovered many of their weaknesses, but there's always more to learn."

Jack's face lit up with immediate interest.

"Do you think you could get close enough to sabotage their weapons and create confusion among the troops? If they start to distrust one another and turn on each other, it would be to our advantage."

Even in his human form, the predatory grace of Chess's demonic feline side showed through. "It would be my pleasure to cause such chaos among them."

"I can infiltrate their dreams," Ransom volunteered. "I can gather intelligence without being seen or heard by the living."

"I'm rather good at deciphering codes," Winston chimed in. "If anyone can bring me that information, I can unravel its true meaning."

"Perfect," said Jack. "You three focus on gathering intel on the Red Queen's army. Meanwhile, Queen Amari will research spells that could free the Jabberwocky from the Red Queen's control. We need every bit of information you can find."

"What about me?" Hatter asked. "How can I help?"

"Your fae magic will be put to good use by helping me create traps for Roxanne's army," Callister answered, his voice strained from the effort of speaking.

Jack shook his head.

"You're in no physical condition to be digging holes and hanging up nets in the forest. I'll take Hatter to meet with some of my captains, and we'll take care of the traps."

Callister scowled, then lit a cigarette with a shaky, wrinkled hand. "What am I supposed to do? Sit in a rocking chair and wait by the fire with a good book and a glass of wine? I think not."

Jack put his hands on his hips, pursing his lips as he thought for a moment.

As each person offered their thoughts and suggestions, I found myself growing increasingly anxious. How could I contribute meaningfully to this conversation when my own powers were still so unrefined? The last bits of magic I'd done since coming back to Wonderland consisted of cleaning vampire cum from my running shorts, and turning a glass of water into a vodka tonic.

I wasn't exactly an up-and-coming sorceress.

Finally, Jack's hands left his hips and he folded them across his hard, broad chest.

"Shifters such as yourself are connected to elemental forces, aren't they?"

Blowing out a puff of greyish-purple smoke, Callister lifted a dull brow.

"Yes."

"Perhaps you and Alice could go into the woods

and listen to the whispers of the wind or the murmurs of the earth to learn the movements of Roxanne's soldiers?"

The ancient-looking caterpillar deadpanned for a second, then let out a contemptuous laugh. He flicked his ashes onto the stone floor, then glared at Jack with his pale, watery eyes.

"Do I look like someone whose ears are in any shape to hear something as quiet as wind whispers?"

Hatter and Chess barely managed to smother their laughs. Even I couldn't help grinning.

Callister was probably as deaf as a doorknob.

"Not particularly," Jack replied through tight lips. "How are your feet?"

"Still attached."

"Surely you and Alice can walk around the forest with a puff cannon and plant echoferns along the Red Army's patrol routes."

"That works," Callister said, his cigarette bobbing in his chapped lips. Jack nodded in approval.

"Good. I'll have one of my soldiers outfit you both with a long-range cannon and as many echoferns as you could possibly need."

I opened my mouth to protest my assignment before thinking better of it. Jack wasn't an idiot. He knew there were fuzzy pink bunnies in the woods. And he knew that bringing along Callister was about as useful as escorting a hundred-year old man.

Yeah, I had questions.

Questions like how the hell was I going to defend Callister in his continuously weakening state? How was I supposed to defend myself from flesh-eating bunnies while also lugging a cannon through a forest? These never-ending questions were careening through my head.

But as I'd told Ransom earlier in the meeting . . . I was still getting used to how things worked in Wonderland.

"You should head out immediately," Jack told Ransom and Chess, his expression serious. "Gather as much information as you can. We will meet back here in two days' time."

"Stay hidden and stay safe," Amari added. "It's of utmost importance that none of you are captured. And remember—communication is vital. Good luck."

"Piece of cake," Ransom smirked, his recently recharged incubus powers radiating a sense of confidence that set me at ease. "We'll be in and out before they even know we're there."

"See that you are," Winston murmured, his brow furrowed with concern as he gathered his notes. "We can't afford any surprises."

"Trust us," Chess purred, his grin wide and wicked. "I haven't led you astray yet, have I?"

As Chess and Ransom left the room, I couldn't help but feel a sense of dread settling over me.

What if something went wrong? What if our plan wasn't enough to defeat Roxanne? My thoughts raced, but I knew there was no turning back now. Wonderland needed us, and I was determined to do whatever it took to save it.

I shifted my gaze to Jack and Hatter, who stood

side by side, their eyes locked on a group of figurines, a cluster of soldiers painted in red. Jack's chiseled features were tense, his pale hair gleaming in the dim torchlight. Hatter's typical mischievous grin was replaced by a more focused expression as he adjusted his hat.

Suddenly Jack was at my side.

"Are you ready for this?"

"Uh . . . not really," I admitted.

"You don't have to go on this mission, Alice. You can stay here, where it's safe. I'll send someone else to accompany Callister."

I smiled up at him, touched by his concern. "And leave all the glory to you? Not a chance. This is my fight too. If you honestly think I can handle this mission, then let me prove it to you. Let me prove it to myself."

Jack's sharp gaze softened, and he nodded in agreement.

"Very well. Come with me, and I'll get you all the equipment you'll need."

CHAPTER
EIGHT
ALICE

The thick forest loomed before me and Callister. Snow-covered branches reached up into the pale gray sky like evergreen towers. I'd traded my cropped sweatshirt and running shorts for more tactical winter coat and boots. Jack had given us something called a 'snowbrush,' which looked like the train of a dress, but ensured that our tracks in the snow would be swept away, leaving no trace that we were ever there.

Our mission seemed simple enough—plant the echoferns along potential enemy patrol routes and around the outskirts of villages, creating a network of magical devices that would transmit sounds and light back to Amari.

If everything went according to plan, the echoferns would pick up on conversations and send back holograms of the Red Army's movements. Knowing their plans would bring us one step closer to victory.

In the far distance, the sounds of battle reverberated through the trees, an ominous reminder of the looming danger that threatened our world.

But here, in this quiet sanctuary, the main sounds that greeted our ears were the soft whispers of the wind in the branches and the muted rustle of creatures scurrying about their business.

The weapon I carried was as intriguing as it was bizarre. It resembled a small potato gun, with its wide barrel and simple trigger designed to launch ammo with barely a whisper of sound. I gripped the puff cannon tightly, my knuckles whitening around the handle, and glanced over at Callister.

"Are you absolutely positive that we don't have to worry about the fuzzy pink bunnies?"

He gave me a weak, yet sly grin, then nodded.

"Yes. It's their breeding season. They're all busy fucking in their underground burrows."

My shoulders sagged in relief. I hadn't seen any tracks, but they were sneaky little fuckers.

Callister motioned at the satchel of echoferns slung over my shoulder.

"We're getting close to some of the Red Army's patrol routes," Callister murmured, his eyes scanning the treeline for any signs of enemy movement. "Do you remember how to load that thing?"

"I think so." I reached into the bag of echoferns and took one out, examining it in my fingers. It was a tightly wound ball of green, like a big marble made of moss. It pulsed with a dormant energy, just waiting to be activated. Once it was planted and matured, we'd have ears everywhere.

"Grab a handful. You should always load multiples, in case you miss your target," Callister advised in his dry, wispy voice. "Even if your aim is true, it's still less suspicious to see large clusters of ferns than one or two."

"Got it." I dropped the echofern back into the satchel and grabbed as many as my hand could hold. Then I loaded them into the puff cannon's chamber just like Jack had shown me back at the military fort. I turned to Callister. "Where am I aiming?"

"Nowhere, yet. Hand it over."

I offered the puff cannon to him for inspection, then watched as he locked the chamber in place and nodded in approval.

"*Now* you're ready."

"Whoops. Sorry about that."

Despite his hunched back and slouching posture, Callister managed to shrug.

"You're still learning. The worst that would've happened is the echoferns could've spilled out and be wasted."

"I'll remember to lock the chamber next time," I assured him. "Where am I supposed to shoot these things at?"

Slowly, he lifted a hand and pointed far off in the distance to a path of dirty, melted snow.

"There. Anywhere along that path."

I squinted at the distance.

"I dunno . . . that seems *really* far away."

"It *is* really far away. There's no need for us to risk getting any closer," he said, sounding like a curmudgeon. "Use the scope, then squeeze the trigger."

"Are you sure we're close enough to hit our target?" I asked, my eyes darting between the puff cannon and Callister.

"Alice . . . stop second guessing everything and just shoot the damn thing. We have a lot of ground to cover."

"If you say so."

With careful precision, I nestled the cannon against my shoulder and gazed into the small scope, then took aim down the winding path. I squeezed the trigger, and the cannon expelled a muffled puff of air near my ear, launching the little green balls deep into the snowy underbrush along the path.

Over the next few seconds, delicate green fronds rose up and unfurled, blanketing the area with magical transmitters that would help us spy on our enemy.

Callister's gravelly voice broke the silence. "Nicely done. If you keep that up, we'll have the entire eastern perimeter lined by the end of the day."

"This is way easier than I was expecting," I said, more to reassure myself than anything else. "Roxanne's army won't know what hit them."

"Don't jinx it," he warned, his voice low and serious. "Keeping one step ahead of Roxanne requires constant vigilance, and we still have a long day ahead of us."

"I know, I know," I conceded, my finger poised on

the trigger once again. "But I can't help feeling like we've totally got this in the bag."

He shot me an exasperated, old man scowl.

"Alice! What did I *just* tell you? Stop talking like that, or you'll jinx us."

"Yes, sir," I smirked. I gave him a mock salute as I slung the puff cannon slung over my shoulder like a soldier's rifle. My optimism wouldn't be so easily squashed.

We moved stealthily through the forest, stopping every so often to plant another inconspicuous cluster of echoferns. The puff cannon emitted a satisfying 'thwump' as it launched each round into the ground. The forest floor was soft and springy under my boots, the powdery snow muffling our footsteps while the snowbrush dragged behind me, making them disappear.

As we worked our way towards the outer villages, I couldn't help but feel that our mission would be a breeze. A strange sense of exhilaration coursed through me.

I was actually helping!

My heart thumped in joy at the simplicity of our mission. Plant a few ferns, get out quickly. Cover your tracks. Repeat. No need to worry.

"We're just outside the village of XYZ," Callister said, his haggard, wrinkled face creasing with a smile. "Ready to plant some more?"

"Absolutely," I replied, unable to contain my own grin.

"Over here," Callister whispered, guiding me off

the faint trail. "The echoferns should take root and blend in seamlessly with the foliage."

I nodded in silence, brushing away a cobweb that clung to my face as he pointed to a large well near a gnarled, ancient oak tree.

"Stand back," I whispered, lifting the puff cannon scope to my eye. With a muffled 'whoosh' and a trail of glittering green pollen, the little balls sailed through the air and embedded into the trunk of the tree and the base of the well.

We worked through the afternoon and early evening, planting our auditory landmines like little seeds of rebellion.

After searching for a place to camp for the night, Callister paused and turned to face me. "Here. This spot will do." He began unpacking a small bag, then scattered a bit of dust on the ground all around our feet. The snow thawed, and a circle of woody vines grew up and up, weaving into a little makeshift hut.

A large mushroom pushed out of the dirt, swelling until it was thick and fat and big enough for him to sit down on.

I set the puff cannon on the ground and joined him.

"Everything about this mission seems too easy," I said under my breath, watching as Callister pulled a handful of mushroom and ate a bite of it. "Something isn't right."

He made a derisive sound, halfway between a growl and a hiss.

"I warned you—don't say things like that, or you'll jinx us."

I shook my head and kicked off my boots.

"Your paranoia is getting really old, old man. Why do you have to be such a worrywart? We'll be fine! We haven't run into any trouble all day!"

"Stop saying that!" he croaked.

Suddenly a twig snapped in the woods beyond our hut. Callister kept complaining but I froze in place. My heart leapt into my throat as the sounds of footsteps and clanking armor grew louder, accompanied by harsh voices.

That's when Callister finally heard it.

We were no longer alone.

We exchanged a panicked glance, but there was nowhere to run.

The walls of our hut were slashed with axes and swords until there was nothing left. Cold dread shot through me as the forest exploded with movement all around us. Half a dozen of Roxanne's soldiers materialized from the underbrush, harsh laughter erupting as they swiftly encircled us with blades drawn.

A towering brute of a man pushed through the ring of soldiers, an ugly sneer twisting his face. "Well, well, well. Here I thought we weren't going to find much on our scouting mission, but it appears we've struck gold. I guess the worm and his whore crawled a little too far from the White Queen's castle."

I grabbed the puff cannon and took aim, ready to unleash a storm of green fury.

"Drop it, little doe, or the caterpillar gets it,"

another gruff voice behind me growled. A dagger was pressed against Callister's wrinkled, tattooed neck.

My heart sank as I lowered my weapon.

The soldier in front of me guffawed loudly, clearly relishing Callister's inability to fight.

"Going to introduce me to your lady friend, worm? Such a pretty little thing." His piggish eyes raked over me lecherously. The name's Kronsk."

I turned my head away in sheer disgust.

"Holy shit—what do you guys use for toothpaste? Dirty diapers?"

Kronsk laughed, revealing a row of half-rotten teeth. "You're a feisty one."

"Fuck you!"

"Aw, you can count on that," Kronsk said, wagging his fat finger at me.

In an instant, we were swarmed by Roxanne's minions. Their grip on my wrists was like iron, their foul breath hot against my neck as they bound my wrists with cold, unforgiving manacles.

They started to drag me away, and I kicked out while I had the chance—not at the soldiers, but at the puff cannon. The chamber fell open and a few little green balls rolled out and landed on the ground. Amidst the chaos, I seemed to be the only one who noticed the soft fronds of two echoferns rising up to witness our fate.

"Callister!" I screamed as he was met with the same fate, but my cry was cut short by a rough hand over my mouth.

"Don't kill her!" he begged the soldiers.

"No need for that." Kronsk leered at me as his men slowly closed in. "The Queen wants her alive...for now at least. Can't make any promises about the condition either of you will be in when she's done with you though."

I watched in horror as they took turns punching Callister's frail body, easily subduing my friend and lover. Violet blood dribbled from his ear and mouth. His insect and snake tattoos writhed in pain, too weak to defend him or fight back. Callister's faded, watery eyes met mine, and I saw what looked like an entire lifetime of pain and regret haunting their depths.

"Alice..." The word was little more than a tortured rasp. "I'm so sorry..."

The soldiers brutalized him until he fell limp and unmoving. Only then did they finally relent, gathering up his battered elderly body like a hunting trophy. Kronsk swaggered towards me, that same mocking grin etched on his rugged features.

"Quit that squawkin' and whimperin', girlie. I'd hate to have to gag that pretty little mouth of yours. Not before the Queen's had her fun at least." He leaned in uncomfortably close, his rancid breath like a punch in the face. "She has...very special plans for you."

With those grim words still lingering in the air, our captors hoisted us onto their shoulders and carried us through the shadowy forest.

The soldiers' camp emerged through a break in the trees, with countless rows of tents lit up by smaller fires. A bigger fire burned at the center, where a much more beautiful tent stood.

If you could call it beautiful in the first place.

I don't think it ever was.

The red flag at the top was half rotted away, and splotches of mold stained the outer walls so badly that I couldn't imagine what the inside looked like. The reek of mildew wafted out of it, making me want to gag.

But I recognized the pattern, because it was the same one adorning the soldiers' armor.

"Your Majesty, we come bearing gifts," Kronsk announced to the group settled in around the largest fire.

The soldier carrying me set me down, my bare feet landing on squishy, moldy mud. I looked over at the group to see a tall, angular woman among the brutes. Her once-beautiful face was now twisted into a grotesque parody of its former self. Veins bulged beneath paper-thin skin, and madness danced in her eyes.

But the moment I saw her blood-red lips twisted into a triumphant sneer, I knew exactly who I was looking at.

Roxanne.

My stomach dropped as she emerged from her

throng of minions and stepped within inches of me. Her gaze settled on my own, her eyes glinting with malice. I had no idea she'd already made it this far into Amari's kingdom.

"Well done, Kronsk," she murmured while tracing the hilt of her sword with a gloved finger. "It appears that a pair of meddlesome insects have wandered into my web."

Callister hissed in defiance, his snake and spider tattoos lashing out with a sad fraction of their old vigor. Roxanne flicked them away and laughed before taking off her gloves. She ran a talon-tipped nail down my cheek, relishing in my shiver of revulsion.

A tall soldier spoke up, his voice dripping with pride. "Caught them planting echoferns along our patrol routes."

Roxanne's grin widened, revealing sharp, cruel teeth. "How disappointing," she said, feigning sympathy. "I expected better from you two." She turned her attention to Callister, her eyes narrowing. "You're going to pay for your insolence...slowly. And painfully."

"You've been . . . a very naughty girl, haven 't you, Alice?" she purred, her breath reeking of rotting flesh. "All you had to do was stay out of Wonderland . . . but you just keep coming back. I suppose I'll have to punish you with methods that you'll understand."

"Leave her alone, you despicable cunt!" Callister spat, writhing against his captors.

"Oh, Callister . . . that's no way to address your queen," Roxanne cooed before sauntering over to the caterpillar shifter. "You'll pay for that."

I watched, helpless, as she plunged her nails into Callister's shoulder, evoking a gargled scream from him. She withdrew them, coated in his violet blood, and licked her fingers clean. "Delicious, my pet. But not nearly as delicious as your screams will be."

She signaled to her minions, and they dragged him off to one side, leaving me face-to-face with the Red Queen.

"Now, where were we?" Roxanne smirked, firelight dancing in her eyes. "Ah, yes. Your punishment. Perhaps your punishment should be my soldiers' reward."

With a flick of her wrist, my coat and fleece leggings were magically stripped away, leaving me naked and exposed and shivering in the freezing winter air. All that was left were the iron manacles holding my wrists together.

"Kronsk . . . when was the last time you, or anyone in your scouting party knew the pleasures of a woman's flesh against your own?"

Kronsk's men whispered among themselves. "It's been some time, my Queen," he replied.

Roxanne lifted an ugly eyebrow at him.

"Then today is your lucky day. Take your pleasure however you see fit, but don't kill her."

"No," I whimpered. "Please, don't."

Roxanne's smile grew even crueler. "You should've stayed away from Wonderland when you had the chance, Alice. And how can I deny my men the pleasure of your company? After all, one must celebrate their victories, shouldn't they?"

Kronsk threw down his axe and dropped his pants, revealing a swollen shlong that shouldn't have been humanly possible. He advanced on me, licking his lips.

"No!" I begged. "Roxanne, please... I'll do anything—"

"Too late for that now," she replied, running a claw-tipped finger down my spine, sending shivers of revulsion through me. "Your time for bargaining has passed."

Kronsk yanked me by my hair, forcing me down to my knees, and I gagged as the putrid stench of his unwashed dick and balls filled my senses. Crying out, I thrashed, but it was no use—he was too strong.

"That's right, sweetheart," Roxanne purred. "Fight all you want. It'll just make it better."

He shoved himself inside my mouth, the girth of him stretching me to the point of breaking. I gagged again and again, until I'd puked onto his groin.

It didn't stop him.

Sick fuck didn't even take pause.

"Such... spirited prey," Roxanne cooed. "I'm going to enjoy watching my men break you."

As the first assailant pummeled my mouth, two more soldiers grabbed me from behind, forcing my knees apart.

"No—" I screamed, but my cries were muffled by the cock in my mouth.

They didn't even bother to prep me. They just... pushed, relentlessly, mercilessly, their girths tearing through the meager defenses of my pussy and my ass. The pain was blinding, white-hot agony that threatened to consume me.

"Yes," Roxanne purred. "Take it, you filthy whore. Take every inch of my men."

On it went, my cries muffled by the invader in my mouth, my body violated in every way possible. As one would pull out, another one would take his place, an endless procession of crude, angry cocks, thrusting hard, each one more painful than the last.

At first I tried to fight back, bucking and thrashing against their hold, but they were too strong. And with each thrust and slap on my skin, I could feel my body giving in to the pleasure that came despite the pain.

My world collapsed into an existence of throbbing and pumping . . . of pain and humiliation as I endured the abuse. Meanwhile, my body continued to betray me by becoming slick with arousal, easing the way for my attackers.

"See? She likes it. Such a good little slut," Roxanne moaned as she watched her soldiers use me like a Fleshlight. Her hand was beneath the skirt of her armor, her wrist moving as she stroked her own clit. "Look at you, drenched in their filth.

And I was.

My body was a mass of new bruises and fresh

cum. My ass and pussy ached, but still, they continued, driving home their dominance with each brutal thrust.

"You were made for this, weren't you?"

I wanted to scream at Roxanne that this wasn't what I was made for—that I was more than just a wet hole for her sadistic soldiers—but all that came out of my mouth were moans and cries as they continued to rape me.

Through it all, I could see Callister being forced to watch at knifepoint, his eyes filled with pain and despair.

"Callister!" I wailed, my voice echoing through the Red Army's encampment. Those who had gathered for the gruesome spectacle simply stared in perverse fascination, their expressions devoid of any sympathy. Some of them began jerking off, eventually using my face as target practice for their spurts of putrid cum.

Just when I thought I couldn't take any more, they abruptly stopped and pulled out of me, then moved away. My body trembled with exhaustion. My mind was numb, hardly aware that I was drenched with wet, sticky cum of at least two dozen strangers as I lay there on the cold ground.

I focused on the bright orange flames of the fire, oblivious to the frantic movements of the soldiers. Their shouts were like nails on a chalkboard, and I blocked out what they were saying. All I wanted in that moment was for death to claim me.

Little did I know that Death was already among us.

And he hadn't ridden in on a pale horse.

He'd arrived in his terrifying suit of white armor, with the force of his army and my wicked boys behind him. I caught sight of his demonic horned helmet, and a pair of blood-red eyes glowed with the fires of vengeance.

Jack.

My White Knight.

My heart leapt as our eyes connected, a silent understanding passing between us. He had come for me.

He would end this nightmare.

CHAPTER NINE

JACK

The moon hung low in the sky, casting eerie shadows across the Red Army's encampment. The sounds of anguished screams and malicious laughter grated against my ears as Ransom and I moved silently through the forest. We passed a large cave with a narrow opening, and I turned to face the troops behind me.

To my left and to my right, Amari, Hatter, and some of my best soldiers were waiting for my signal to attack, ready to unleash madness and chaos against our enemies.

We had them surrounded, and they didn't even know it.

We were close . . . so close . . .

But not close enough to attack without losing the element of surprise.

"If we have to retreat, head for this cave," I said, motioning to the dark jagged opening.

My army nodded in silence.

The cold night air nipped at my skin, but I hardly felt it. Adrenaline coursed through me, sharpening my senses, fueling my determination. We had received word from Amari about Alice and Callister's desperate pleas for help through the echoferns, and I'd wasted no time gathering enough troops for our rescue mission.

"We can't wait much longer," Chess said from somewhere in front of me. All I could see of him were his emerald eyes, but I didn't want him to make himself more visible until it was absolutely necessary. He'd scouted ahead and quickly found Alice and Callister's location. "I don't know how much more abuse Alice can take."

I picked up the pace, knowing that if I moved any faster, I might snap a twig and give away our ambush. When the trees finally parted, my blood boiled in fury at what I saw.

Alice was shackled and pinned to the ground by half a dozen men, helpless to stop them from rutting into her from both ends. Callister, bloodied and bruised, was being forced to watch.

I clenched my fists, outrage rising up within me. The monster within was snarling to break free, fueled by a primal urge to protect what was mine.

"Careful, Jack," Ransom cautioned in a low whisper, "We can't afford to be reckless now that we've found them."

He was right, but with each second that ticked

by, I could feel my patience wearing thin. I tightened my grip on the hilt of the Vorpal Sword, the enchanted blade that could cut through anything.

"Alright," I whispered, my voice laced with a promise of violence. "We strike fast and hard, then get Alice and Callister out of here."

Ransom nodded, his eyes filled with a similar deadly determination. As we prepared to launch our attack, I took one last glance at Alice and Callister. Their pain and fear fueled my resolve, and I knew that nothing would stand in my way of saving them.

"Ready?" I asked Ransom before glancing at Queen Amari.

"Ready", Ransom replied, his eyes never left the horrific scene folding out in front of us.

The Queen whispered "ready", clutching the hilt of her sword.

Hatter's gaze of his mismatched eyes didn't need to answer, he was ready for madness, and most of all, vengeance.

"Draw your weapons," I whispered to Hatter, Ransom, and our soldiers. Without a sound, they unsheathed their swords, the blades glinting with silvery light in the darkness. Ransom shifted into his demonic form, his black wings pinned close to his body to conceal the crossbow he'd brought along.

Those soldiers ravaging Alice would know the true meaning of suffering before I granted them the mercy of death.

Almost there . . .

Just a few more yards to go.

The stench of mold and rotting flesh assaulted my senses . . . the scent of darkness and evil. The scent of the Red Queen's source of magic.

We were seconds away.

I held my breath, then gave the signal to attack.

With a fierce battle cry, we charged into the camp —Amari, Ransom, Chess, Hatter, half the White Army, and myself.

The Red Queen's soldiers scrambled for their weapons, but it was too late. Our patience had paid off, and we had the upper hand. My sword sliced through the air, decapitating the first man I encountered before he could even scream.

His head thudded to the ground, blood spurting from the severed neck. I lunged for the next soldier, piercing his heart in one swift thrust. He crumpled without a sound.

I wasted no time going after the first two soldiers who had been raping Alice. In a flash of cold steel, their heads tumbled to the ground. Blood sprayed in a graceful arc, splattering onto my helmet and across my armor, igniting my bloodlust.

I spun around, the Vorpal Sword glinting in the moonlight as I continued my assault on the other men who had dared to defile my precious Alice. With each swing of my blade, the blinding fury within me intensified.

No one could touch me.

I moved too fast for mortals to see. Even demons had a difficult time tracking my movements.

"Look who decided to join the party," one of the soldiers sneered at me. He was a hulking brute with his belt still unfastened below his fat belly. He lunged at me, his sword raised high above his head. In a swift and brutal motion, I plunged my blade into his gut, ripping it upward and watching as his intestines spilled out onto the ground. The man's eyes widened in shock and pain, and I reveled in his suffering.

It was the best deliverance of justice I could give Alice for the crimes he'd committed against her.

"Is that all you've got?" I taunted as I turned toward my next opponent. The spear-wielding soldier charged, but I sidestepped their attack and swung my sword downward in an arc, severing their arm at the shoulder. They screamed, cradling their bloody stump as they collapsed to the ground.

I cut and slashed my way through the melee, not stopping until I'd personally avenged Alice by ending the lives of every man who'd touched her.

The last soldier who'd defiled her backed away in terror from me, his hands raised in surrender.

"Please!" he begged. "Have mercy!"

"There is no mercy for those who harm the innocent." My voice came out cold and hard as I stalked towards him.

He screamed and tried to flee, but I was faster. With a swift stroke of my sword, I sliced him in half from shoulder to hip. His internal organs tumbled out in a gruesome mess as his torso flopped to the ground.

A scream tore through the air.

Roxanne.

I whirled around, sword at the ready, to find my companions pulling down the largest tent at the center of the camp. Amari's hands glowed with the full power of her magic. Ransom's claws dripped venom, and Hatter's eyes gleamed bright with madness.

And Chess . . .

In the blink of an eye, he shifted into his giant, fearsome form, towering over the battlefield like a nightmarish specter. His body shimmered as it became semi-transparent to avoid injury. His fingers elongated and grew into enormous paws, allowing him to easily tear through flesh and bone with razor-sharp claws.

His fur was instantly mottled with blood, but it only seemed to make him more terrifying. He prowled forward on silent paws, taking out half a dozen soldiers with every swipe of his claws. And all the while, his Cheshire grin stretched from ear to ear, his wide rows of razor teeth on full display.

The Red Queen shrieked again, scrambling backwards and flinging spells to deter us. Her magic splintered against Amari's palms, then ricocheted off Chess's fur.

As I fought my way closer, I could see the desperation in the Red Army's eyes—the knowledge that this might be their last stand. It only fueled my rage, driving me to fight harder, faster, more ruthlessly than ever before.

If this was the battle for Wonderland, I would not let her down; I would not let her fall.

"Jack, I'm over here!" Alice screamed as another wave of soldiers closed in around her and Callister. The sound of her voice was like a jolt of electricity, spurring me to cut down anyone who dared to stand in my way.

"Hold on, Alice!" I roared, my sword slicing through the air as I cleaved through one enemy after another.

The battle raged around me, our forces clashing with a cacophony of metal and magic. Amari fought valiantly against Roxanne's dark sorcery, her own spells shimmering in the air as she struggled to match her sister's power.

"Ha-ha! Let's dance, gents!" Hatter cackled, unleashing bursts of his chaotic fae magic that sent Roxanne's soldiers scrambling in confusion.

"Chess, keep their forces at bay!" I commanded. He gave me a wicked grin in response.

I watched in satisfaction as he unleashed the full strength of his demonic powers upon our enemies. His feline agility was unmatched as he twisted and turned through the chaos like a wraith. Soldiers screamed and fell around him, their bodies shredded and mangled.

Ransom flew above the chaos, picking off men one by one with his crossbow. Bodies fell like tin soldiers being knocked over by an invisible hand. There were so many men lying on the filthy ground that they were becoming a trip hazard.

"Jack!" Hatter shouted, his voice tense. "On your left!"

I turned just in time to see a soldier lunging at me with his sword raised. With a snarl, I parried his attack and plunged my blade into his chest, watching as the life drained from his eyes. Another soldier took his place, but he met the same fate, his blood mixing with that of his comrade on the forest floor.

"Keep going!" I yelled, pushing forward through the sea of soldiers, my eyes locked on Alice and Callister. If I could just reach them, everything would be alright.

The screams of soldiers echoed through the night as I severed limbs and carved open torsos. Blood sprayed in every direction, warm and sticky against my armor and gloves. With each slash of my sword, bone shattered and muscle tore, the scent of blood filling the air like a visceral perfume. My rage fueled me, driving me to kill without mercy or remorse.

"Nice work, Jack," Ransom shouted from the air above me, grinning wickedly as he raised his cross bow and took out another soldier. "But we've got more incoming."

The metallic scent of blood filled the air, and the cries of pain and fear from Roxanne's soldiers amplified my fury. I was death incarnate, an avenging force for Alice and Callister.

"Push forward!" I roared to my army, my voice laced with vicious rage. "Do *not* let them stop us!"

I swung the Vorpal Sword without hesitation, decapitating a soldier as he tried to block my way. His head rolled to the ground, blood spurting from his severed neck in gruesome arcs.

My next target was a powerful soldier attempting to skewer Hatter with a spear. Using supernatural speed, I intercepted the attack, impaling the man through the chest with my sword. His eyes widened in shock before I unceremoniously ripped the blade out, leaving his lifeless body to crumple to the ground.

"Thanks for the assist, Jack," Hatter said, his grin never faltering despite the carnage surrounding us. "These assholes really know how to throw a party!"

"Stay focused!" I snapped, knowing that any distraction could be fatal.

As I moved through the battlefield, my vampire instincts guiding my every move, I spotted two soldiers cornering one of our own against a tree. Without a second thought, I leapt into the fray, slicing through one soldier's throat so deeply that his head nearly detached from his body. The other barely had time to register my presence before I plunged my sword through his abdomen, entrails spilling out as he screamed in agony.

"Go! Rejoin the others!" I barked at the grateful White Army soldier, who quickly disappeared into the fray.

"Jack, we're making progress!" Amari called out, her voice strained from fighting. "But Roxanne's magic is stronger than I anticipated!"

The stench of blood and fear filled the air, a miasma that clung to my senses as I surveyed the battlefield. Our forces were holding their own, but it wasn't enough. We needed an edge, something to tip the balance in our favor.

Alice and Callister's lives depended on our success.

"Move forward!" I roared, urging my soldiers on. My senses were heightened to an almost unbearable degree, every movement and sound registering in excruciating clarity. My heart raced, and I reveled in the carnage around me, the vampire's bloodlust driving me to even greater heights of brutality.

"Jack, we're losing ground on the left flank!" Ransom shouted, his voice strained as he fought against the tide of enemy troops.

"Focus your attacks on their weakest points! We need to break their line!" I replied, my mind racing as I analyzed the situation. I could see the uncertainty in my soldiers' eyes, but I knew I had to lead them through this hellish chaos if we stood any chance of reaching Alice and Callister.

"Amari, can you reinforce our defenses?" I asked, hoping that her magic could turn the tide in our favor.

"I'll do my best, Jack," she responded, her brow furrowed in concentration as she cast a series of protective spells around our warriors.

"Keep pushing! We're almost there!" I encouraged my comrades, my voice a thunderous roar above the din of battle. My sword whipped through the air, severing limbs and cutting down foes with brutal efficiency. I didn't revel in the gore, but it was a necessary part of this fight.

"Damn it, they just keep coming!" Hatter's manic laughter filled the air as he continued to unleash his chaotic magic, but even his wild energy seemed to be wearing thin.

"Chess, how much longer can you keep this up?" I inquired, concern lacing my voice as I watched the giant Cheshire Cat demon tear through our enemies with a savage ferocity.

"Long enough!" he replied, his breath ragged from exertion. "We can't let them win!"

"Three more soldiers coming your way, Jack!" Ransom called out, his voice strained from the effort of holding back Roxanne's dark magic.

"Let them come!" I roared, my eyes blazing with an unholy light as I charged towards my new opponents. They seemed to hesitate for a moment, taken aback by my unnatural ferocity, but that hesitation cost them dearly. My blade tore through flesh and bone, severing limbs and heads with ease, leaving nothing but mutilated corpses in my wake.

"Is that all you've got?!" I screamed into the night, daring any other fools to challenge me. My heart ached for more blood, more destruction, but something deep within me knew that I couldn't afford to lose myself to this frenzy. Alice and Callister were counting on me.

"Jack, look out!" Amari's voice rang out through the chaos, snapping me back to reality just in time to dodge a deadly swing from an enemy soldier. I was grateful for her warning, but there was no time for thanks as I countered with a vicious strike of my own, decapitating the attacker in one fluid motion.

My fury burned like the fires of hell as I continued my relentless assault, hacking through enemy after enemy. The once lush forest was now a blood-soaked battlefield, littered with dismembered limbs and lifeless bodies. But even as the Red Army soldiers fell to my sword, it seemed as if their numbers never dwindled.

"Retreat!" Roxanne's shrill voice carried over the din of battle. "Take Alice and Callister and fall back!"

"Damn her!" I growled as I saw Roxanne, holding a battered Alice by the arm, while her soldiers dragged an unconscious Callister along. I desperately fought against the tide of Red Army soldiers blocking my path, but for every one I cut down, three more took their place. Deep down, I knew we would lose ground if we didn't act fast.

We need to push forward!" I shouted, struggling to be heard above the clashing of steel and the screams of the dying. They responded with fierce determination, unleashing their powers upon our enemies in a desperate attempt to break through.

"Jack, we're trying, but there's too many of them!" Ransom roared, his demonic form tearing through soldiers like paper.

"Keep going!" My teeth gritted, I continued to

fight, knowing that with every passing moment, Alice and Callister were slipping further away.

"Look out!" Ransom's warning reached me just in time, and I narrowly dodged a stream of blazing flames that erupted from the monstrous jaws of a hideous beast above me.

The Jabberwocky, a nightmare made flesh, swooped down from the sky, its massive wings casting eerie shadows on the ground below. Its eyes burned with malevolent intelligence, and its razor-sharp claws gleamed with deadly intent.

"Stay close!" Hatter yelled, unleashing a torrent of magical energy towards the creature. But the Jabberwocky merely snarled, swiping at the air with its fearsome talons, unharmed by his assault.

"Chess, can you get us close enough to strike?" Ransom asked, his demon powers crackling through the air as he readied himself for battle.

"I'll try," Chess replied, shifting into his giant Cheshire Cat demon form. His body became semi-transparent, and he leaped towards the Jabberwocky with feline grace. We followed suit, our weapons ablaze with power, determination etched on our faces.

"Amari, keep our men safe," I commanded, my voice laced with concern. She nodded solemnly and began weaving protective spells around the remaining soldiers.

As we clashed against the Jabberwocky, I felt a surge of adrenaline course through my veins. My vampire bloodlust was fully activated, granting me the strength and speed to face this monstrous adversary. But despite our combined efforts, it became increasingly clear that we were outmatched.

"Jack, we can't keep this up!" Hatter shouted, his eyes wide with panic. "We're losing too many men!"

"Fall back! To the cave!" I ordered, gritting my teeth against the agony of defeat. I knew it was the right call to make, but the thought of leaving Alice and Callister behind filled me with despair. My heart ached for them, and my rage towards Roxanne knew no bounds. I longed to sink my teeth into her throat and drain her life away, to make her pay for what she had done.

Furthermore, the realization that we were no match for the Jabberwocky tore at my resolve like its serrated claws. How could our army ever compete when the Red Queen commanded such a beast?

Chess managed to shield us as we retreated, but many of our soldiers weren't so lucky. Screams filled the air as the Jabberwocky's fiery breath engulfed them, turning their bodies into charred husks. The weight of their sacrifice bore down on me, as heavy as the beast's heated flames.

As we retreated through the forest, I glanced back one last time at the devastation left in our wake. The once peaceful woodland now resembled a scene from a nightmare, the earth soaked in blood and littered with the broken bodies of friends and foes alike. It was a stark reminder of the cost of our failure – and a bitter taste of the horrors yet to come.

Once safely in the cave, I slumped against the

cold stone wall, my heart aching with loss and frustration. We had failed to rescue Alice and Callister, and now we were trapped, hunted by a monstrous abomination conjured by Roxanne's twisted magic.

"Jack," Amari said softly, placing a gentle hand on my shoulder. "We'll find another way."

"Another way?" I spat bitterly. "Every time we get close, she slips through our fingers. And now... this." I gestured towards the chaos outside the cave, the screams of the dying still echoing in my ears.

"Roxanne wants us to break," Ransom said, his voice low and steady. "She wants us to lose hope. But we won't give her that satisfaction. We'll regroup, and we'll come back stronger than ever."

"Damn right we will," Hatter agreed, his madness momentarily tempered by the gravity of our situation.

I nodded, clenching my fists in determination. No matter what it took, I would bring Alice and Callister home.

The air in the cave was stifling, thick with the scent of fear and charred flesh. I pressed my back against the cold stone wall, trying to keep my breath steady as the Jabberwocky's monstrous shadow loomed outside the entrance, its guttural growls shaking the earth beneath us.

"Any ideas on how to get out of here?" Hatter asked, his voice tense but still tinged with that signature madness. His eyes darted around the cave, searching for an escape route that didn't exist.

"None," Amari whispered, her face pale as she clutched her staff tightly, her knuckles turning white.

"We simply have to wait until my sister calls her Jabberwocky to return."

"We could make a run for it," Hatter suggested. I didn't know if he was joking, or if he was starting to lose his grip on reality.

"Amari is right," Chess said weakly, wincing as he shifted his injured arm. I hadn't noticed his injuries while he was covered in fur and blood, but now that he'd gone back to his human shape, his injuries were more obvious. "We need to stay calm until the Jabberwocky leaves. It's our only chance to get out of here alive."

As if on cue, the Jabberwocky let out a furious roar. Its massive claws scraped against the ground just outside the cave.

The knowledge that we were trapped like rats in a cage gnawed at me, fueling the anger and desperation simmering beneath my skin. My thoughts raced, trying to piece together a plan, but every idea seemed more futile than the last.

We were just going to have to sit here until it was safe to move.

And as Supreme Commander of Queen Amari's White Army, I wasn't accustomed to doing nothing. My chest tightened as I thought about Alice and Callister, who were being taken further and further away from us by the Red Queen's army.

The oppressive weight of the Jabberwocky's presence seemed to stretch time into an eternity. When it finally took flight with a thunderous beating of its massive wings, I felt a surge of adrenaline course through me.

"Now!" I hissed.

And even though it nearly killed me to do so, we fled the safety of the cave and pushed through the darkness until we arrived back at Amari's castle.

The cold stone walls of Amari's castle offered no comfort as we regrouped after our failed rescue attempt. If anything, her icy fortress seemed to echo our collective despair.

The dim torchlight flickered in the drafty corridors, casting eerie shadows across our faces. Each of us wore the weight of our failure like a heavy cloak, our expressions etched with grim determination. I paced back and forth, trying to come up with a solution.

"We could bring our entire army to the Red Queen's castle," Winston suggested.

"That's exactly what the Red Queen wants," I said through gritted teeth, my hands clenching into fists at my sides. "Her forces are too powerful. We can't simply rush into battle again . . . not while she possesses such dark magic. We barely escaped with our lives this evening."

"I know, I know," Winston sighed in frustration. "But we can't just sit here while Alice and Callister are suffering at the Red Queen's hands!"

"Then what do you propose?" Chess asked, his voice low and gravelly. His injuries had left him weakened, but the fire in his green eyes still burned brightly.

"Perhaps we could train more soldiers?" Winston suggested.

I shook my head.

"We've already recruited nearly every eligible fighter left in Wonderland. There aren't many people left who haven't already fallen under the Red Queen's control or been hunted down by her forces."

"Perhaps," Ransom suggested hesitantly, "we could send Chess to rescue them? He can disappear at will, after all. He could sneak into the Red Queen's castle undetected."

All eyes turned to Chess, who grimaced in pain. Although Amari had treated his injuries, it was clear he was still in a moderate amount of pain. "I... I can try," he admitted reluctantly, "but my magic isn't fully restored yet."

"How long will it take?" Ransom asked. "Would a good night's sleep do it?"

Chess let out a rare contemptuous laugh.

"As if I could get a good night's sleep after what we've just gone through. No . . . I'll need at least two days. Maybe three. But . . . "

Ransom lifted a brow.

"Go on."

"Even if it only takes me two days to recover, and even if Alice and Callister are still alive when I get to the Red Queen's castle, it's not likely that I'd be able to save both of them."

The room went silent, the weight of Chess's words hanging heavily in the air. Each of us knew what it meant.

In his aged, elderly, weakened condition, Callister was essentially dead weight. Even with Alice's help, he would only slow them down.

Nobody said a word. Nobody wanted to be the one to decide which of our friends to save, and which one to leave behind.

CHAPTER TEN

ALICE

Dread pooled in my gut as the Red Army marched Callister and I through the dark forest. The air was thick with tension and fear. Every step we took brought us closer to a fate worse than death.

The sounds of snapping twigs and rustling leaves filled our ears as we trudged onwards, with the looming presence of Roxanne's castle growing ever closer. The atmosphere was suffocating—each breath I took felt like I was inhaling poison.

My overconfident, cocky declarations of how easy our echofern mission was had jinxed us into being caught. I couldn't shake the deep remorse I felt at bringing all of this horror and death upon us.

Not only was I to blame for what those disgusting soldiers did to me, and not only had I led Callister to his death, but I'd also baited Amari and Jack and all of my friends into a hopeless battle against Roxanne's forces.

All because of me.

I'd walked us straight into Roxanne's trap, blind to the danger. How could I have been so stupid? So reckless? Now Callister was going to die for it, and Wonderland would remain under The Red Queen's tyrannical rule.

If only I could take it all back, undo my foolish mistakes. But it was too late. I'd failed Queen Amari and all of my wicked boys.

I'd failed all of Wonderland.

There seemed no escape from the bleak darkness closing in around us, as inevitable as the breaking light of dawn.

Callister trudged beside me, his usual swagger replaced by a painful limp and a grim resignation. Despite my shackles, I reached for his wrinkled, tattooed hand, my fingers brushing his.

Fresh tears stung my eyes.

"I'm so sorry for jinxing us and getting us into this mess."

He gave my hand a weak squeeze. "Don't blame yourself, Alice. You were only trying to help." His tired smile was sad but genuine. "At least we're together at the end. I never wanted to die alone."

"Is there anything we can do?" I asked in a hushed tone, knowing full well that the soldiers around us could be listening. "Anything at all?"

"Do whatever it takes to stay alive," he replied, his voice low and serious. "If you can find a way to escape, take it and run . . . and don't look back."

The tears welling in my eyes fell down my cheeks, landing on my violated, naked, cum-stained tits. How could I leave Callister behind? The thought of abandoning him to Roxanne's psychotic schemes made my stomach churn.

Internally, I screamed at myself to find a solution, to come up with some brilliant plan that would save both of us from our awful fate.

We marched all night until the Red Queen's castle loomed before us like a nightmare. The darkness that clung to the structure seemed to seep into my very being, filling me with a sense of impending doom.

Its twisted spires clawed at the sky like skeletal fingers of black stone. Its dark, mold-covered walls were dripping with slime and covered with dark, thorny, twisted vines that seemed to writhe in the shadows. The oppressive air grew heavier as we approached, and I could practically feel the evil energy pulsating through every brick and stone. A sense of foreboding washed over me, chilling my blood and causing my heart to race.

Suddenly Roxanne was standing in front of us. Her hideous, warped expression was pulled into a sadistic grin.

"Take the caterpillar to the town square," she ordered the soldiers closest to him. "He dies at sunrise. Don't kill him before I get there."

Panic flooded my senses as the scouting troupe of soldiers passed Callister over to another pair of men.

He struggled in vain against their grip, but his old, frail body was barely more than wrinkled skin and brittle bones.

She stepped forward, tilting my chin up with one gloved finger.

"And you, my dear Alice, will have the privilege of watching his head roll from the dungeon." Her smile was venomous. "Perhaps then you'll learn not to interfere in my affairs."

Bile rose in my throat. This was all my fault. If I hadn't insisted on carrying out this stupid mission . . . if I hadn't jinxed us. Roxanne gave me a rough shove toward her soldiers, her eyes glittering with malice.

"On second thought, don't bother taking her to the dungeon. Take them both to the town square. Alice's day of reckoning has arrived."

As we were led past the dimly lit outer walls of the castle, the eerie decorations added to the unsettling atmosphere. Gargoyles leered down at us from their perches, their twisted faces contorted into expressions of pure evil.

Shadows danced along the slimy walls, cast by flickering torches that offered little warmth or comfort. Mildew-covered fountains spewed endless streams of what seemed to be a combination of piss, pus, and liquified shit.

"Can't say I'm a fan of her decorating choices," Callister quipped, trying to inject some levity into the situation. But his words fell flat, and the tension between us remained palpable.

Our footsteps echoed off the cold stone floors as we were brought to the center of the town. Every step brought us closer to our doom, and I could feel the weight of despair settling on my shoulders.

"Listen," Callister whispered urgently, breaking the suffocating silence. "If it comes down to it, I want you to run. Just leave me behind and find Amari. She'll know what to do."

"Callister, don't say that," I pleaded, my voice shaky. "I can't just abandon you."

"Promise me, Alice," he insisted, his eyes filled with concern. "Please."

"Fine," I choked out, my throat tight with emotion. "I promise."

As we neared the outdoor execution platform, the shouts and jeers of the crowd gathered outside reached our ears. The Red Queen's subjects were eager for blood, hungry for the spectacle that awaited them. I wasn't surprised, given that they were willing to live in a town that oozed rivers of shit and slime.

Maybe Roxanne's particular brand of evil magic had corrupted them to a point where they simply didn't care.

My heart raced as I desperately searched for any sign of an escape route. But I was surrounded by hordes of Roxanne's loyal subjects. They jeered and sneered, closing in on us like a pack of hungry wolves.

The execution platform loomed before us, a grimy scaffold of bloodstained wood and rope. An executioner's block sat in the center, stained dark with old blood. My stomach churned at the sight, then lurched again as Roxanne climbed to the top and waved to her people.

"People of Wonderland! Behold, two of our most vile traitors!" Roxanne announced, her voice dripping with sadistic glee.

At that moment, the soldiers seized our arms, dragging us up to join Roxanne on the platform. I stumbled along the steps as they hauled me past crowds of jeering onlookers. In the gloomy grey of dawn's first light, I caught a glimpse of Callister's face, pale with dread.

Despite the his frail bones, sagging skin, and the immense pain he must have been experiencing, he refused to show any weakness. Still, I'd seen the terror in his eyes. He was afraid, although he would never show it.

She gestured to Callister and me, her crimson lips twisted into a cruel smile. "This one conspired with the enemy to overthrow me. Who among you is ready to witness the consequences of defying your rightful queen?"

The crowd roared with approval as Callister was shoved forward to the chopping block, stumbling on legs so tired and weak that it was a wonder they still functioned at all. A cold sweat broke out across my brow as I watched him struggle to stand tall.

I swallowed hard, staring at the floor of the platform to avoid meeting anyone else's gaze. My heart pounded, and guilt twisted my insides into knots, followed swiftly by a wave of nausea. We were going to die together, side by side, all because of my stupidity.

Callister glanced over his shoulder until he caught my eye. His skin was becoming so thin and fragile that it almost looked transparent. He was aging so quickly that his eyes were sinking into his skull, yet in that fleeting moment, I glimpsed understanding. Forgiveness. No blame or anger. Only a quiet acceptance of what was to come.

This was it, then.

This was the end.

"I didn't hear you! Who's ready for the executions to begin?" Roxanne's voice rang out, cruel and cold as ice. Her question was met with so many screams of excitement that I wondered if these were even people down there.

To me, they were all monsters.

Satisfied with the volume of their response, Roxanne conjured an ebony throne and took a seat, tapping her blood-red nails on the armrest as a smug smile curled her lips.

Trembling with rage, I summoned a burst of magic in a last-ditch effort to kill the fucking bitch. But before I could launch it at her, Roxanne batted it away with her hand as easily as shooing away a fly.

"None of that now," she scolded, wagging a finger at me. "I've waited much too long for this day. You'll not spoil my fun now that it has arrived."

Roxanne raised her hand, and the crowd fell silent as if on cue, their collective breaths held in anticipation. Two guards forced Callister onto his knees, pulling his shoulders down until his head was resting on the chopping block. His arms and legs seemed to crumple from their brutal handling.

Roxanne gave a nod, and the executioner stepped forward, his axe glinting in the sunlight. The crowd drew a collective breath.

"Watch closely, Alice," she said with the most evil grin I'd ever seen. "Watch while I take from you the one thing you have left in this world."

She swung her arm down, signaling for the executioner to carry out his grisly task. "Off with his head!"

"NO!" I screamed as I lunged towards Callister, but strong hands gripped my arms, holding me back. Tears blurred my vision as the executioner's blade sliced through the air, severing Callister's head from his body with brutal efficiency. The crowd gasped in shock, and my screams of despair filled the air.

"NO! NO! Oh Callister!" I sobbed, my heart breaking into a million jagged pieces as his decapitated head rolled to a stop on the ground.

No.

No, this couldn't be happening. It was all some horrific nightmare. Any minute now, I'd wake up in my bed in Malibu, surrounded by fuzzy pink pillows.

Fuck—I'd even be glad to be back in that hospital bed, if it meant Callister was still alive.

But I couldn't argue with the very real sight of his bashed in head being kicked around like a football by the townspeople below. It appeared hollow, dried-out, shriveled, and misshapen, an unnatural mockery of the vibrant friend I knew and loved.

"Your turn, dear," Roxanne taunted. Her eyes were filled with perverse satisfaction as I was dragged forward. She reveled in the horror and despair that consumed me, feeding off of it like a ravenous beast.

"Please, don't do this," I begged. "I'll do anything you want."

"Too late for that. You sealed your fate when you chose to defy me," she purred, her cold fingers tracing circles on the arm of her chair. She shook her head in disappointment. "I didn't ask for much, Alice. All I wanted was for you to stay away from Wonderland."

"So you could take it over like a plague! I hope you rot in Hell, you fucking cunt!" I spat, my grief transforming into a white-hot rage. If this was my end, then I would face it head-on just like Callister had . . . refusing to give Roxanne the satisfaction of seeing me cower.

"Such fire!" she laughed from the comfort of her throne. "Pity it's about to be extinguished."

Shaking with anger and horror, I stumbled over Callister's body and had my head forced down onto the block where his had been just seconds earlier. The rough wood scraped against my cheek, and I knew it would soon be stained with my own blood.

I focused my eyes down at Callister's body, wanting him to be the last thing I saw.

Roxanne had won, and all hope was lost.

The executioner turned to me, his axe dripping with violet blood. Ignoring him, I kept my eyes firmly on Callister's body, and my stomach churned at the grotesque sight of a giant green maggot pulsing inside his torso. It writhed and squirmed, moving like the blue pills that had invaded my kitchen. I fought back the urge to puke as the maggot rippled and moved inside Callister's skin.

"Let it be known," the Red Queen proclaimed, her voice dripping with venom, "that Alice Darling, the so-called savior of Wonderland, has committed heinous crimes against our realm and its rightful ruler, myself!"

A long list of false accusations spewed forth from her lips like bile, each lie more twisted and outrageous than the last.

Illegal use of shrinking and growing potions.

Disrupting her croquet game.

Stealing one of her favorite tarts.

Painting her roses red.

As tears welled up in my eyes, I couldn't stand to hear any more of her bullshit.

"Oh for fuck's sake, none of that is true!" I yelled out, my voice barely audible above the jeers of the bloodthirsty crowd. "If you're actually gonna kill me, just hurry up and get it over with!"

"Very well," Roxanne sneered, nodding to the executioner. "Give this traitor the death she deserves."

As the axe was raised high above my head, I took one last look at Callister's pulsating body, filled with the giant fat green maggot, then squeezed my eyes shut. My heart pounded like a drum, drowning out the cruel laughter of the crowd as fear and regret warred within me.

"Long live Wonderland," I murmured.

Suddenly the crowd broke out in screams. My eyes snapped open to see a sudden burst of lime green and turquoise moth wings exploding out of Callister's corpse. Gasps of shock rang out from the crowd as a terrifying humanoid creature rose to its feet and unfurled two sets of long, insect-like arms.

Then it locked its huge compound eyes on mine and reached for me.

I screamed, but with my wrists still shackled, there was no way for me to fight it. The mothman's grasp was firm and unyielding, lifting me off the platform just as the executioner's axe fell onto the empty chopping block, slicing through empty air where my neck used to be.

Relief and disbelief washed over me as the mothman quickly lifted me into the air, far out of the executioner's reach. We rose higher and higher, soaring above the platform while the crowd pointed and shouted from below.

"Shoot it down! Get her back!" Roxanne screeched, her face contorted with rage as she watched her carefully laid plans crumble before her very eyes. "Don't let them escape!"

But the mothman ignored her, its wings beating furiously as it carried me up into the sky above the execution platform. My heart hammered in my chest, pumping adrenaline through my veins as Roxanne and her archers launched a flurry of arrows and blasts of magic spells at us.

The mothman responded with an agile swerve, narrowly avoiding assault from the Red Army below. It seemed to possess an uncanny sense of timing, anticipating each attack before it reached us. Fear and relief warred within me, unsure whether to trust this savior borne of my worst nightmare.

If this creature dropped me, I'd have to be taken off the ground with a power washer.

The wind howled around me as the mothman's powerful wings sliced through the air, carrying us higher and farther away from the horror unfolding below. I couldn't help but shudder at the memory of Callister's lifeless, hollow body lying on the execution platform.

My heart ached with guilt, and my mind raced, trying to understand how he could have had this creature living inside him all this time . . . this creature that was now holding me in its scratchy legs.

Below us, Roxanne's enraged screams cut through the chaos, her voice shrill with rage. "You will not escape me, Alice Darling!" she shrieked. "I will hunt you to the ends of Wonderland!"

Her screams grew fainter, her fury a distant echo in the vast expanse of sky that was now between us. And even as the mothman soared higher into the clouds, I knew that our escape would not go unpunished.

The Red Queen's vengeance would be swift and brutal.

Her threats sent a cold chill down my spine, but it was what followed that truly struck terror into my heart. A thunderous roar shook the air, drowning out the wind and the clamor of the crowd.

And as soon as I heard the sound pierce the sky, I knew the Red Queen's chosen method of vengeance was the very definition of swift and brutal.

It was the Jabberwocky.

CHAPTER ELEVEN

ALICE

The moment I glanced over my shoulder, I instantly regretted it.

The Jabberwocky, Roxanne's most fearsome monster, a creature of nightmare and destruction, had risen from a plume of red smoke and was hurtling towards us through the clouds at alarming speed. Its vast wings were so huge that they were casting a dark shadow over the landscape below.

I screamed as jets of flame shot out from the hideous demon's nostrils.

"The Jabberwocky's right behind us!" I screamed at the mothman. "You have to fly faster!"

The giant insect carrying me seemed to understand the urgency in my voice, its wings beating even harder as we raced through the sky. But the Jabberwocky was relentless, hot on our trail, its roars shaking the air like rumbles of thunder.

"Please, whoever you are . . . whatever you are," I sobbed, praying to whatever this thing was that had saved me from the chopping block, "please, just get us out of this nightmare alive!"

The clouds enveloped us, and for a brief moment, the Jabberwocky seemed to vanish.

Suddenly a blast of searing heat shot towards us, nearly singing my hair. I shrieked, cowering in the mothman's hard, skinny legs as the Jabberwocky unleashed another jet of fire at us. My heart leaped into my throat, mentally preparing myself to be engulfed in flames.

The mothman angled into a sharp dive, speeding below the blaze at break-neck speed. The Jabberwocky snarled in frustration, banking around for another attack.

The mothman's wings beat furiously as it dove downward, cutting through the cloud cover before plunging into the forest, narrowly weaving between massive tree trunks.

A dense woodland stretched out all around us, an untamed wilderness of tangled branches and ancient trees. Our descent was swift, and I could hardly catch my breath as we plunged into the shadows. The Jabberwocky crashed after us, snapping branches and tearing foliage.

I squeezed my eyes shut, bracing myself for the beast to grab us in its claws at any moment.

"Are you insane?!" I shrieked, holding on tighter to the mothman's powerful arms. "You're gonna kill us!"

It didn't respond, but its movements were calculated. It darted between the trees with grace and precision, narrowly avoiding obstacles that threatened to tear us apart.

The Jabberwocky roared in frustration, its thunderous voice echoing through the forest like a furious storm.

"I think you're slowing it down! Keep going!" I urged the creature holding me, though I doubted it understood my words. "Don't let it catch us!"

The mothman didn't need my encouragement – it kept zipping between the trees and dense undergrowth, its vibrant wings reflecting the dim light that filtered through the canopy above.

Bursts of fiery breath lit up the darkness behind us, a constant reminder of the Jabberwocky's relentless pursuit, until it let out an ear-splitting screech. The mothman fluttered close to the ground, dropping me onto a giant mushroom.

I sank into it like a memory foam cushion and watched as the green and teal blue creature folded its large wings behind its back. My heart pounded as I stared at my rescuer, still not quite believing that either of us were alive.

The longer I studied his appearance, the less scary he actually looked. He was just . . . unexpected.

Two long, fuzzy antennae swiveled on top of his head, swaying gently in the breeze, moving like big bunny ears in search of sounds.

His deep teal green eyes were enormous for a human, but pretty normal by moth standards. His body was a mix of hard muscles covered in armor-like exoskeleton and soft fur, a strange combination that made me long to reach out and touch him. Instead of fingers at the end of his four long arms, he had long, spiny digits that were more like talons. No wonder his grip was like being trapped in a vise.

And underneath the fur, crawling around the surface of his exoskeleton, were fresh tattoos of insects and snakes that I instantly recognized.

"Callister?" I breathed, hardly daring to hope. "Is that you?"

The mothman let out a laugh.

"Were you expecting someone else?"

"Holy *shit*!" I screamed in disbelief. "You're alive!"

"Barely," he said with a familiar smirk.

Even through the insect face, that smirk hadn't changed a bit.

Joy and relief flooded through me as I threw my arms around him, clinging to him tightly. Tears of gratitude and happiness spilled down my cheeks. After witnessing his execution, I could hardly believe he was alive and carried me to safety.

"You're alive," I whispered over and over. "You're really alive."

He hugged me close in his four long, fuzzy arms, his heart beating steadily against my ear through his exoskeleton. "Thanks to you," he said softly, gazing at me with his huge insect eyes. "You helped stall for enough time for me to shed my old skin. Just a few seconds less and I couldn't have done it. You saved me."

I smiled, wiping away my tears before I looked up

at him. "And you saved me in return. I guess that makes us even."

Callister grinned. "Not even close. You don't owe me anything." Then his voice grew rough with concern as he looked me up and down. "Are you alright?"

I gave myself a once-over, searching for any gaping wounds. I was scratched up from tree branches and covered in dirt and sweat and cum and blood spatters from the battle where Jack and Amari had tried to save us . . . but overall . . . I was alright.

Whatever 'being alright' even looked like.

The more time I spent in Wonderland, the more the definition seemed to keep changing.

"I've been better," I muttered, not ready to remember the horrors I'd lived through in the last twelve hours. "At least I'm not dead."

Callister's moth-like face turned even more serious. "We should get out of here before Roxanne or her soldiers find us again."

As if to prove his point, a deafening roar shook the air, and a dark shape caught my attention.

The Jabberwocky.

My blood turned to ice at the sight of its fiery eyes and gnashing teeth as it struggled in the grip of powerful tree limbs. It was lodged in there pretty good, and the more it thrashed against the dense foliage, the more it was entangling its massive form.

A heavy dead tree limb groaned and fell on its head. The limb rolled halfway down its neck, trapping the beast in place. I instinctively cringed at the sounds it was making. Even though it was trapped and couldn't move, the creature was terrifying.

But beneath the rage, I sensed something else—

Pain.

Agonizing, endless pain.

A memory of Ransom's voice drifted into my innermost thoughts.

Demons do feel pain, Alice, no matter their outward form . . .

I took a deep breath, steeling my nerves as I took a few steps closer.

I hadn't noticed until now that the Jabberwocky was wearing a collar. I squinted in the shadowy forest light, not knowing if what I was looking at was real.

But it was.

The collar was embedded with long, sinister spikes that were digging into its scaly flesh, tearing ragged holes in the Jabberwocky's thick hide. Deep orange blood oozed from the wounds, dripping like liquid fire from its neck.

The poor thing. No wonder it was so full of rage.

The Jabberwocky might've been a scary-as-fuck demon, but was suffering all the same.

Suffering because of what that repulsive cunt Roxanne had done to it. She was still doing it, even now, when it needed her help the most.

I couldn't walk away knowing it was being tortured like this.

"I'll be right back," I said to Callister. He opened his mouth to argue, but stopped short of saying anything. Maybe he'd seen the worry in my eyes.

Whatever the reason, he nodded and followed silently behind me as I slowly approached the trapped demon.

Summoning my courage, I raised my hands in a peaceful gesture and adopted the goofy, non-threatening voice I've always used when I'm talking to dogs.

"Hey buddy, I'm not gonna hurt you, okay? I'm here to help."

The Jabberwocky's slit-pupiled eyes fixed on me, glowing with rage and suspicion. But it held still, letting me come closer without protest.

"Aww, that's a good Jabberwocky," I said, still talking in my dog-approved voice. "Look at who's such a good demon. Let's get that icky nasty collar off your pretty neck, mmm-kay?"

I could see the exact moment when it registered that I meant it no harm. The malice faded from its gaze, replaced by wariness. And maybe, just maybe, a glimmer of hope.

It let out a high-pitched whine, and my heart ached at the sound.

"No creature deserves to suffer like this," I said to Callister. "Not even a monster."

"You'll get no argument from me."

"Don't worry buddy . . . I'm gonna get this thing off of you." I was finally close enough to get a good look at the collar. The spikes were barbed, designed to cause maximum pain with every movement. Even breathing must've been agony for the poor beast.

With infinite care, I started working the first

spike out of its flesh. The Jabberwocky growled and thumped its tail like an angry cat—a humongous, angry cat—but it let me continue my work. Eventually Callister made his way around its massive, tangled body and started removing collar spikes from the other side.

Droplets of fiery orange blood pooled around the spikes as I eased them out one by one, letting them fall to the forest floor with a metallic thud. By the time I pried the last spike free, the Jabberwocky's neck looked like it was dripping with molten lava.

Only the metal band of the collar remained, fastened in place with what looked like a giant railroad spike. Although I was able to lift the giant iron nail out of the clasp, there was no way I could pull off the heavy metal collar.

"Callister, can you help lift the collar off from over there?" I asked across the demon's thick, scaled neck.

"Sure. I'm going to push it over to your side," he answered. "There's something in it that you ought to see."

"Okay, sounds good."

I took a few steps back, then watched as Callister used all four of his arms to hoist the collar off the Jabberwocky's neck and fling it over its body in my direction. It bounced off the leaves and rolled a few yards away. But all I could think about were the wounds on the demon's neck.

My mind raced as I desperately tried to think of a way to help it. I closed my eyes and summoned the image of a bandage covered in a healing salve, willing it into existence with all my might.

I opened my eyes, and saw a long roll of white gauze covered in thick purple paste. With trembling hands, I carefully placed the bandage over the deep puncture wounds on the Jabberwocky's neck.

The monster let out a low growl, but seemed to relax as the healing magic of the purple salve seeped into its skin. The air was thick with tension as I worked, every movement calculated and deliberate.

The last thing I wanted to do was piss this thing off.

A strange sound rumbled in the Jabberwocky's chest. It was the first sound I've ever heard it make that didn't scare the shit out of me. Its voice was deep and gravelly, but there was a warmth to it I never expected.

That's when it dawned on me—

It was *purring*.

"Are you hearing this?" I whispered to Callister as he sidled up next to me and folded his two sets of arms over his exoskeletal chest.

"I am," he replied with a bewildered nod that made his antennae bounce. "I had no idea the Jabberwocky could make such a sound."

I finished my work and took a step back. The Jabberwocky seemed lighter now, its eyes softer, scales gleaming with vibrant color instead of sooty black. It was beautiful in its own way, this strange creature of nightmares and shadows.

Callister waved me over to where the collar still lay on the ground. Then he pointed down at it.

I immediately noticed something I hadn't seen before on the massive metal collar: it was adorned with a large ruby. The color of it was unmistakable – it belonged to The Heart of Wonderland."

"Is that . . . is that what I think it is?" I asked, even though I already knew the answer. There was absolutely no way that jagged stone of rosy red could be anything else.

"I'd bet my life on it," said Callister.

"We have to bring this back to Queen Amari," I murmured under my breath. I stooped down and picked up one of the collar spikes from the ground, then used it to pry the ruby out of the collar. I picked it up, mesmerized by the radiant glow that filled my palm.

"I don't have any pockets," I said, looking at my battered naked body.

"You have the power to fix that," Callister told me. "You have more power than almost anyone else in Wonderland right now. You can do a lot more than conjure a pocket."

I bit my lip, glancing at my bare skin before looking at the trapped Jabberwocky nearby. Despite the danger, I knew what had to be done.

Cradling the ruby in both of my hands, I gazed into the soft, bright red light and thought about what I wanted, what I needed more than anything else in this moment.

I need those trees and bushes to set the Jabber-

wocky free. I don't want the Red Queen to have control over it anymore. Let the Jabberwocky return to wherever it belongs . . . wherever it wants to be. The Jabberwocky is free.

The ground rumbled and shook as the trees groaned, twisting and bending apart as their branches unraveled the wooden cage holding the demon in place. The Jabberwocky growled and thrashed, and Callister pulled me into the safety of his four arms.

Together we watched as the Jabberwocky emerged from the twisted maze of branches and foliage. It spread its majestic wings and took flight, rising up into the sky.

Its scaled body glinted in the sunlight, casting an eerie shadow over us as it soared away with a powerful beat of its leathery wings. The rustle of leaves and the creaking of branches echoed in its wake, leaving Callister and I behind, staring after it with a sense of wonder.

After a long moment, he turned to look down at me.

"What did you do?"

"I told the Jabberwocky that it didn't belong to anyone. That it was free."

He brushed my cheek with one of his long, hard fingers.

"I don't think I know of anyone in all of Wonderland who would've been brave enough to do what you just did."

I shook my head and let out a dismissive laugh. "I'm not that brave."

"Yes, you are," he insisted, still holding me against his hard, fuzzy body. "That's one of the things I love about you."

His words cut me to my core, and if we hadn't been all alone in a forest, I would've automatically assumed I'd misunderstood him.

But I hadn't.

"You . . . you really mean that?"

"Oh Alice," he whispered, his voice a low rumble that sent warmth flooding through my body. Still holding me, he guided us over to a massive fallen log and leaned against it. "I mean every word. I thought I might never get the chance to tell you how much you mean to me. I'm glad the plan worked."

I raised a curious brow at him.

"What plan?"

He grinned wickedly at me.

"The plan to stave off my metamorphosis until the very last possible moment."

My jaw fell.

"Why didn't you tell me that was the plan all along! I thought you were dead! I was bawling my eyes out!"

He gave a remorseless shrug. "It had to look real. I couldn't take the risk of us getting caught."

I wagged my finger in his face, pretending to scold him.

"You naughty, naughty caterpillar."

Grasping my finger with two of his strange, bony arm protrusions, he shook his head.

"I'm not a caterpillar anymore. I won't be for quite some time."

I looked up at him, taking in the soft, velvety texture of his wings and the way they cast eerie shadows on the ground beneath us. Despite the monstrous appearance, there was a strange beauty to him that I couldn't help but appreciate.

"How long will you look like this?"

My curiosity got the better of me, and I reached out to touch the feather-soft tufts of fur that grew from the gaps of his exoskeleton. He made no move to stop me.

"I can shift into my human shape whenever I want," he explained, leaning into my caress. "But it feels so good to simply exist in my true form...to have you near me, and not be afraid."

"How could I be afraid? You're beautiful," I breathed, utterly enchanted by his surreal appearance. Callister's wings were unlike anything I'd seen before. Each scale was edged in silver, fading to opalescent lime greens and aqua blues toward the center.

I found the chinchilla-soft fur between the insect parts of his body both exotic and alluring. I drank in every detail, from the iridescent edges of his blue and green wings to the rhythmic flutter of muscles as they shifted under my curious touch.

A low, gravelly purr rumbled in Callister's chest, startling me. "Not many would call a creature like me beautiful," he said, a wry note to his tone. "But I'm glad you think I am."

Heat rose in my cheeks as I realized I'd been gawking at him, running my hands over his body like I couldn't get enough of his strange softness. But Callister didn't seem to mind my fascinated exploration.

A quiet groan escaped him, and I froze.

"Should I stop?"

"No," he said with a wicked laugh. He shifted against the fallen log, leaning down to nuzzle my throat with his fuzzy antennae. "Don't stop," he rasped, nipping at my ear.

A jolt of desire shot through me at the touch of his mouth and the vibration of his purr against my skin.

I swallowed hard, arousal and nerves twisting in my belly.

"Callister . . . "

"Yes?"

"I . . . I don't want . . . " I hesitated, torn between my fascination with him and the fear that what I wanted to tell him was too twisted, too wrong to say out loud.

"Tell me, Alice. You can say anything you want to me."

I hung my head, staring at the filth . . . the ugliness . . . the bruises on my body. Then my eyes flickered to meet his, my words hanging heavy in the air between us.

"I don't . . . I don't want some disgusting soldier to be the last person that fucked me," I stammered as I gazed into his infinite insect eyes.

"I want it to be you. I want you to make the pain go away."

"You want me to heal you?"

I nodded, and he slowly spun me in a circle within his four arms. When I was facing him again, the dirt and blood and cum and scratches had been erased from my skin. My body appeared as rejuvenated as if I'd just stepped out of a spa. Even the bruising on my inner thighs had disappeared, along with the raw pain in my core.

I swallowed hard, knowing there was just one more thing I wanted to ask.

"Say it out loud," Callister told me, his eyes holding mine with an intensity that made my heart race. "Say what you want and I'll do everything in my power to make it happen."

A shiver ran down the back of my neck and my nipples hardened at his words and the promise they held. I didn't understand this desire for a giant moth, but I'd loved fucking the caterpillar. Surrounded in his hard softness, I was helpless to resist his allure.

I licked my lips, knowing that once I made my request, Callister would definitely be able to make it happen.

"I want you to fuck me . . . but not too hard. And I want you to come inside me. I want you to wash away any trace of those other men."

Callister groaned, the sound vibrating through his chest where he held me close. His wings fluttered and wrapped around us, cocooning us in shadows and the earthy scent of moth dust. Dipping his head down again, he nipped at my throat once more in a possessive gesture.

"Nothing would please me more," he murmured, and began repositioning my body in his four spindly insect arms.

His antennae brushed against my bare skin, the soft fuzz tickling my tits and belly before sliding lower. I gasped as he traced swirling patterns over my crotch, coaxing out sparks of pleasure wherever his antennae touched.

"You like that, don't you?," Callister hummed, his voice a low rumble against my ear. "You want me to give you pleasure unlike any you've known before."

He was right. I wanted him in a way I couldn't explain, my body burning for his strange, inhuman touch.

"Yeah," I begged, rocking my hips to increase the pressure of his antennae. Sparks of pleasure burst inside me, my clit throbbing with need.

Callister chuckled, the sound dark and possessive. His antennae slid lower, tracing teasing circles around my entrance before sliding inside.

I moaned at the sensation, so different from anything I'd felt before. His antennae were soft and slick, writhing against my inner walls and stimulating places no human lover ever had.

Pleasure swelled inside me as Callister's antennae moved deeper, stroking and teasing until I thought I might go insane with lust.

"Tell me if I should stop," he said, pulling them out of me.

"Don't stop," I pleaded, thrusting my hips towards his head. "Never stop!"

Callister hissed in triumph, his antennae curling and stroking inside me until I came apart with a scream of ecstasy. Stars burst behind my eyes as pleasure flooded my senses, more intense than anything I'd known before.

My body still shuddered with aftershocks of pleasure as Callister held me against his warm, soft body. Finally I went limp in his arms, panting and dazed from the force of coming so hard. I sank against him, sliding down his silky fur, until his fat cock caught me between my legs and stopped me.

I gazed up at him through half-lidded eyes, captivated by the sight of his magnificent moth wings fluttering with excitement.

"It's the only part of me that doesn't change." I glanced down and adjusted myself to look at the swollen cock waiting patiently for an invitation to come inside.

Just like what I'd seen before, Callister's cock was the most fascinating of all my wicked boys. The narrow tip was a deep shade of emerald, almost inky black, perfectly designed for prying open the tightest of holes. It gradually faded into a lighter hue near the base. Its shape tapered from the sleek, delicate tip to a plump and bulbous middle, before ending in a narrow base. It was the kind of shape that once inside a body cavity, it wasn't going anywhere without some effort. The surface was covered in tiny spiky protrusions that promised intense pleasure on my sensitive clit.

With its intricate ridges and glossy wet sheen, I couldn't wait to get that thing inside me and ride it.

"Are you ready for me?" he asked, his voice thick with anticipation.

"Y-yes," I stammered, unable to tear my gaze away from his pulsing insect cock. It was thick and ridged, yet fat and squishy, designed for maximum stimulation.

"Good girl," he purred, guiding himself into me with one of his lower hands.

As the thickest section slid into me, it caressed sensitive places his antennae had awakened. I gasped at the intense sensation, an intoxicating blend of pleasure and pain, before arching my body into him. Then the narrow base sank into me, lodging his cock in place where it belonged . . .

Deep inside my body.

For a moment we remained motionless, savoring the feeling of our joined bodies. Then Callister began to move, pulling almost all the way out before sliding back in.

"Tell me how it feels to get fucked by a moth shifter," he demanded, his breath hot against my ear.

"I fucking love it!" I admitted, unable to deny the truth as he began to thrust slowly, deliberately. "I love the way your cock stretches me and fills me up. It feels so good . . . but kinda wrong at the same time. Like I'm fucking an alien insect monster."

The feeling was foreign, unnatural even, yet I

found myself craving more. My mind raced with thoughts of how wrong this was, mingling with the undeniable arousal that coursed through every fiber of my being.

"Ah, but isn't that what makes it so deliciously perfect?" he teased, quickening his pace. "The forbidden fruit always tastes the sweetest, doesn't it?"

"Callister, I don't know if I can—" I started, but my words were cut off by a moan of pleasure as he hit a spot deep inside me that made my whole body quiver.

"Let go, Alice. You know you love fucking me when I look like this. Surrender to your most secret desires, and I promise you won't regret it," he whispered, his eyes blazing with a fierce intensity.

He pounded harder and faster into me, his wings beating in rhythm with his thrusts as he chased his release. The soft raised spikes around the base of his cock made an exquisite friction, ratcheting my pleasure higher with each thrust.

I hesitated for only a moment longer before allowing myself to succumb to the darkness, to embrace the twisted passion that burned between us.

Yeah . . . I was fucking a giant insect. And yeah . . . it felt fucked up and delicious and all I could think was that I wanted more. As we moved together, our bodies slick with sweat and lust, I felt a strange sense of freedom in this perverse act.

I glanced down at my pussy bouncing up and down on his slick, swollen cock. The soft fur around the opening kept brushing against my clit, tickling it . . . sticking to it.

Teasing it.

"Oh, fuck, Callister..." I gasped, my body tightening around him as my orgasm approached. "I'm gonna . . . I'm gonna . . . "

"Come for me, Alice," he urged, his voice strained with his own impending release. I could feel the hard knot getting more and more rigid inside me, locking me in place, and I knew what was about to happen.

"Show me the depths of your depravity. Come all over my knot and squeeze the cum out of me."

In that moment, I imagined my pussy squeezing all the juice out of him and drenching my insides, making me his. I let go of all inhibitions, and a powerful orgasm ripped through me, leaving me breathless and trembling in its wake. Callister followed soon after, his own shuddering release filling me with a sticky warmth that seemed to seep into my very soul.

In the throes of our twisted passion, I barely registered the strange sound of a wet pop.

My eyes widened in shock as I realized what had happened: Callister's cock had broken off inside me. I opened my mouth to scream, but he smothered it with a kiss.

"Don't scream, or you'll bring us unwanted attention," he said, waiting until I nodded. "Sometimes this happens. I'll just grow another one. It's part of the process."

"Part of the...?" My voice trailed off as I struggled to reconcile the horrifying reality of the situation. As freaked out as I was, I couldn't deny the fact that I was fascinated by what was happening before my very eyes.

While I sat there straddling him, shocked and speechless, Callister seemed more irritated than alarmed. Sure enough, within a few seconds, a fresh new cock rose from his crotch like those time-lapsed videos of plants growing.

"Let's not waste it, shall we?" Callister said, a wicked gleam in his eyes as he guided the narrow tip of his newly-formed appendage to my ass. The sensation of squishy firmness was exhilarating, and I couldn't help but moan as I relaxed and took him into my ass, deeper, then wider. I leaned forward to push his other cock into my pussy, rocking against the textured spines in a desperate attempt to prolong our depravity.

"Such a greedy little slut you are," he breathed, gripping my hair tightly as he began to thrust in and out of my ass. "How does it feel to have my insect cock in both of your holes?"

"I...I don't even know how to describe it," I mumbled. My muffled words were barely intelligible, but it was clear he understood. The duality of horror and lust within me was tearing me apart, and all I could do was cling to the dark ecstasy and fuck him harder.

"Slow down, or you're going to make me lose

control," he warned, his voice strained with effort as he continued to claim both my pussy and my ass.

But I didn't want to slow down.

I wanted to surrender to the darkness, and let it consume me.

As my pleasure built and intensified, I felt myself slipping further and further away from the world I had once known—a world of rules and boundaries, of right and wrong. No longer did those things matter. All that existed was the primal lust that bound me and Callister together, the insatiable hunger that drove me to fuck him and come on him so hard that he'd broken off his dick inside me.

Fuck . . . it was starting to pulse inside me.

"What's happening?" I asked, slowing down to a stop. I glanced down at the sticky purple cum coating the base of the broken cock.

"Residual cum," he shrugged. "Guess you didn't get it all the first time."

"How is that possible?"

But I didn't have time to wait for an answer. I was suddenly overcome by the sensation of two knots forming inside my body—the residual one from the first cock, and a second knot buried deep in my ass.

"Slow down," he warned a second time. "I don't know if you can handle it."

But the allure of those bumps against my clit were just too tempting to ignore. I started grinding against them, harder this time, as each knot began to swell fatter and stiffer, anchoring me in place.

Callister's cocks swelled further inside me, stretching my walls to the point of pain and pleasure.

Then he went rigid.

"Fuck! Alice!" , screaming as he came in hot, wet blasts that filled me to overflowing. The sensation of seeing his hot purple cum leak out of my pussy and onto his stomach triggered another shattering orgasm in me. I closed my eyes and wailed as I felt my insides twitch and constrict and simultaneously squeeze all they could from both of his hot, throbbing insect dicks.

I was drowning in ecstasy, riding him like a horny little slut, lost to everything but the giant moth shifter fucking me, claiming me so passionately.

Then, with a final moan, he pulled himself free from my well-used holes, leaving me gasping for air. We collapsed onto the forest floor, our limbs entangled and our bodies slick with sweat and iridescent purple cum.

Callister's cum . . . and nobody else's.

I rubbed it into my skin, grinning at the texture, the color, and the scent of him.

"You marked me. I love it. And I love you . . . "

A satisfied groan rose from his chest, and he stirred against me, his soft antennae caressing my cheek.

"Then it's time I left a more permanent mark on you."

"What do you mean?" My question ended on a cry as his hard, bony insect fingers clamped around my right arm. My skin burned with a bright flare of pain immediately followed by the sensation of a bad sunburn. I tried to jerk my arm away but he held me firmly in place. When he let go, I understood what he'd meant by a more permanent mark.

My arm was now branded with a black and teal colored snake tattoo. I glanced down at it and the motherfucker slithered its tongue at me.

"What the fuck?"

"You're welcome," Callister snickered.

"Is it *alive*?" I gasped, unable to look away from the snake writhing on my upper arm.

"She's as alive as you are," he said, dropping his arms down to his sides. "You can name her, if you want."

Two tiny, glittering black eyes looked at me as if she was waiting to be christened. Then her neck flared out on both sides and she started to sway in a rhythm that reminded me of Egyptian belly dancers.

Suddenly I thought of the perfect name.

"I'm gonna call you Jasmine. How's that sound?"

The black cobra danced a few more seconds, then nodded her head.

"We should go," Callister said, rising to his feet and taking me by the hand. "Even if the Jabberwocky doesn't come back for us, the Red Queen most definitely will."

I nodded, not needing to be told twice.

"Let me get dressed first."

I imagined an outfit that was practical, but cute. I'd barely finished my thought and already I was wearing a soft shirt underneath a dark green jacket, sturdy knee-high boots, and sleek black leggings—with pockets that zipped shut.

I walked over to where I'd left the ruby from the Jabberwocky's collar, and slipped it into my pocket, zipping it shut.

"Are you ready?"

I looked at Callister, who had all four arms reaching out for me.

"Oh, are we flying?"

"Yes. It's faster, and safer than walking."

"I thought you'd be exhausted after all that physical exertion," I replied, only half-joking.

Callister shook his head, his antennae bobbing in the air above his furry mothman head.

"It's going to take a lot more than a couple of fucks for me to be exhausted." He pulled me into his arms, outstretched his wings, and pushed off the ground, launching us both into the sky.

"But once we land, you're welcome to try and find out."

CHAPTER TWELVE

ALICE

The air crackled with electricity as Callister and I landed on the roof of Amari's castle. The guards stationed on the ramparts and watchtowers had seen us flying towards them from miles away, and quickly ushered us to safety.

As I stumbled down the staircase and into one of the countless hallways, my heart hammered in my chest. The last time I'd seen my friends, they'd been fighting against Roxanne's soldiers. I didn't know if any of them had been injured or worse.

So the second I clamped eyes on Amari, Winston, Jack, Hatter, and Ransom, I breathed a sigh of relief. Callister and I were filthy, bruised, and exhausted, but we'd made it. They all rushed to greet us, questions flying about our whereabouts. Jack pushed past the others with his supernatural speed and pulled me into his arms, turning the two of us into a tangle of limbs and emotion.

"You're safe," he whispered against my hair, clutching me close.

"Finally," I murmured into his chest. I glanced around, realizing someone was missing. My heart sank. "Where's Chess?"

"He's on another secret mission," Jack replied, setting my mind at ease. "Don't worry. We're expecting him to return at any moment."

"Thank goodness you're both alive," Amari said, leaning against the wall to steady herself. "I thought we'd lost you."

Callister laughed to himself before shifting into his human form.

"It was close. Too close."

Ransom cut in, stealing me away from Jack for a possessive hug of his own.

"What's that hard bulge in your pocket, Alice?" he teased. His hand drifted down my upper thigh until it was cupping the priceless treasure I'd found in the woods.

"Shit! I almost forgot! Look what we found!" I exclaimed breathlessly, pulling the large fragment of the Heart of Wonderland from my pocket.

Ransom's eyes immediately narrowed in disbelief.

"That can't be what I think it is . . . can it?"

"Ohhhh yeah," I gloated as I handed over the glowing red ruby. "I pried it out of the Jabberwocky's collar myself."

"By the stars, Alice," Amari gasped, her eyes widening with wonder as she stepped forward to inspect the stone. "How did you get close enough to do that?"

I shrugged like it was no big deal, but I was grinning my ass off. "I guess I have a way with demons."

"Apparently you do," she gasped, caressing the stone with a trembling fingertip. "This... this is the largest piece of the Heart of Wonderland I've seen since it broke!"

"Yeah, it seems pretty big," I agreed.

"You have no idea how significant this is. With this large of a fragment, we have a real chance to restore Wonderland to its former glory."

We all watched as Amari lifted a necklace over her head, revealing that it held a small white velvet pouch. She opened it and tipped the contents that had been safely tucked inside into her palm. The incomplete Heart of Wonderland was pulsing with energy and magic.

Then it grew even brighter . . . more intense. The piece in Ransom's hands floated up into the air, then began to glow as it seemed to recognize the larger heart-shaped stone in Amari's palm. The two fragments made a beeline for each other, moving and adjusting until they'd reconnected perfectly in place.

A bright rosy red light burned around the broken edge until the cracks disappeared. Only a small handful of chips and fragments were missing. The Heart of Wonderland was almost completely restored.

"You say this newest piece came from the Jabberwocky's collar?" Amari asked.

I nodded.

"My sister knows that the Heart of Wonderland contains the essence of our world's magic, its very lifeblood. She mustn't get her hands on it, but we all know that she will stop at nothing to control the Heart of Wonderland's power." Amari's voice was tight with concern, and her gaze never left the fragment. "We must protect it at all costs."

"Absolutely," Jack agreed.

Ransom nodded. "Without question."

Amari slipped it back into the white velvet pouch and put the necklace back on, tucking the precious jewel against her heart, safe beneath her dress.

Suddenly she looked up at me with tears shimmering in her eyes. "Alice, if I don't survive this war, you may have a larger role to play in the future of Wonderland."

"Me?" I stammered, taken aback. "What do you mean?"

"We don't have to get into all of that right now," Winston said.

Amari shook her bouncy, purple coils. "She needs to know at some point."

"What exactly do I need to know?"

Before Amari could reply, a soft cloud of mist appeared nearby, becoming more and more opaque, until a shadowy figure materialized out of the darkness, making my heart leap into my throat. Chess grinned at our startled expressions, his eyes gleaming like twin embers in the gloom.

My heartbeat quickened at the sight of him.

"Miss me?" he purred seductively. He scooped me into his arms and nuzzled into my neck. "Because I certainly missed you, Alice."

Ignoring the copious display of affection, Jack turned to him expectantly. "Do you have any information about the Red Queen's next move?"

"Yes, tell us, Chess. What did you learn about her plans?" Ransom asked, his expression darkening with every word.

Although his green eyes were glowing with intensity, the grin on Chess's handsome face instantly faded away to a grim line.

"The Red Queen and her forces are already on the move," he explained, his voice heavy with dread. "Her army is massive . . . and they're moving quickly through the forest. She's coming straight here . . . for all of us . . . for Alice . . . and for the Heart of Wonderland. She intends to use the Heart to destroy our world as we know it...." He trailed off, seeming to be at a loss for words. "Lots of shrieking about turning everything to rot and mud and ash . . . and moaning about how she won't stop until all of us are dead."

Panic rose in my chest. We were outnumbered and unprepared. How could we possibly stand against Roxanne's psychotic wrath?

"Then we must make our final stand," said Amari.

"Can we intercept them?" Hatter asked, his fingers tapping nervously against his thigh.

"Yes, but we need to move fast. We don't have

much time," Chess warned. "Roxanne will be here within two days."

"Two days?" I squeaked. I could feel the weight of the situation bearing down on me—on all of us. Everything we had fought for, everything we had sacrificed, was on the line. I took a deep breath, steeling myself for what Chess was about to say next. The urgency in his voice made my heart pound faster.

"Yes. Two days. Maybe less. I've never seen her so furious . . . so dangerous . . . so utterly outraged and unpredictable."

Amari was quiet for a long moment as she let the information sink in. Chess went on to describe complete chaos at the Red Queen's court—soldiers were losing their heads for simply asking questions. The Jabberwocky was missing, and Roxanne's powers seemed to have gone rogue.

"This is good."

My jaw fell in disbelief. "How do you figure?"

"If my sister is this angry, she's more likely to make mistakes," Amari said, her regal composure taking over. "It's time to put the rest of our plans into action. We need to be prepared for anything, and we have no time to waste."

In a whirl of shimmering white silk, she spun on her heel and strode down the hall with Winston, leaving me to wonder what the next steps were.

Jack turned to Ransom with an expectant look.

"Can you get Callister up to speed on our plan for Alice?"

"Of course," he replied, motioning for Callister to join him.

"And you two can work with my soldiers to finish setting the traps," he said to Hatter and Chess.

"What about me?" I asked. "What can I do?"

"If we're going to be prepared," Jack continued, gesturing towards the Vorpal Sword hanging at his side, "then we should have another lesson. A refresher, if you will. Hopefully, it will be our last."

"Good idea," I replied, grateful for something concrete to focus on amidst the chaos of the impending battle. He handed me the sword and led me into a large, dark room, hidden away from the light of day.

"Are you sure you have time for this? I know you've probably got a million things to do, what with you being Supreme Commander of the army and all."

Jack placed a reassuring hand on my shoulder.

"As far as I'm concerned, I only have one task...which is to teach you how to become one with the Vorpal Sword."

I nodded, determination filling my chest as the sword's familiar weight rested in my grip.

"Got it," I nodded, swallowing my fear. "I'll do whatever it takes."

"I know you will," he said with a faint smile. "That's why we're going to win."

For the next several hours, I threw myself back into training with a newfound intensity. I was surprised at how much I remembered.

Under Jack's watchful eye, I honed my skills with

the Vorpal Sword, wielding its power with precision and control. Every swing and thrust sent a thrill of exhilaration coursing through my veins, as if the weapon itself was awakening something fierce and primal within me.

I took a deep breath and swung the sword again, feeling its power surge through me.

And I completely missed my target.

"Focus, Alice!" Jack barked, parrying my blow with ease. "You can't let your emotions cloud your judgment."

"Sorry," I gasped, sweat dripping down my brow. "It's just . . . I'm kinda freaking out right now. There's so much at stake."

"Which is precisely why you need to be at your very best," he reminded me, his blood-red gaze never wavering from mine. "We're all counting on you."

As our blades clashed again and again, I knew he was right. This was no time for doubt or hesitation—not when Wonderland's fate hung in the balance. I couldn't afford to fail . . . not now.

Not ever.

The mood in the Great Hall was bleak at dinner. And that was an understatement. I only stuck around long enough to make myself eat a plate of food before bringing a dreamdew drop cupcake with me back to my room. I needed a break from the chaos that swirled around me.

As I walked down the hallways towards my room, my heart thumped in my chest, drowning out all the other sounds in the castle. The upcoming battle against the Red Queen weighed on my mind like a ton of bricks. I'd trained with Jack as much as possible. I'd studied combat and footwork and various attacks.

Whatever choices I made tomorrow would determine the fate of everyone I loved.

"Forgetting something?"

I glanced up to see Ransom leaning against the wall beside my door. His incubus aura rolled off of him like dark flames. He held two empty wine glasses in one hand, and a large bottle of red in the other.

"Are you sure that's a good idea right now?" I asked, pushing my door open. "Especially when we're on the brink of war?"

Slowly . . . ever so slowly . . . Ransom shook his head before following me into my room with a predatory grace.

"We've been at war for ages. Now is simply the first time you're seeing it up close."

My gaze flicked over to the bottle, and my mouth watered.

"I'm pretty sure Jack wouldn't want me drinking anything."

Unfazed by my concerns about my mentor's unspoken rules of combat, Ransom set down the glasses on my dresser and pulled a corkscrew out of his pocket. Beautiful garnet red liquid splashed into both of the glasses, and he handed one of them to me.

Then he cocked a devilish brow.

"What do you think Jack's soldiers are doing at this very moment, hmmm? They're celebrating what might be their very last moments alive."

I sat down on the edge of my bed . . . a glass of wine in one hand, and a pearlescent, rainbow-frosted cupcake in the other. If this was my last night alive, I might as well enjoy it.

I sank my teeth into the soft cake and frosting, then set the rest of my cupcake on the nightstand. I washed away the sweetness with the tart flavor of the wine, knowing that the clock was ticking.

Tick . . . tock . . .

Tick . . . tock . . .

Tears stung at the corners of my eyes.

"Ransom, can I talk to you?" My voice trembled as the weight of our impending battle pressed down on me. His dark eyes flickered with concern as he took in my anxious expression.

"Of course," he replied, then sat down beside me. I loved how the mattress sank from the inhumanly powerful weight of him. Having him so close made me feel safe. "You can always tell me anything. You know that, don't you?"

"I do," I sighed, running a hand through my hair. "This is all happening so fast. I'm scared shitless that we won't make it out alive."

"Let me tell you something, Alice," he murmured, pulling me close and resting his chin on top of my head. "We're all scared, but we've faced worse odds before."

"You have? I thought this is the worst that Roxanne has ever been in the history of Wonderland."

Ransom gave an unconcerned shrug.

"Well . . . it is . . . but we have the upper hand."

"How do you figure?" I whispered, seeking reassurance in his embrace.

"We have *you*," he replied, his breath warm against my ear.

"It's so much pressure." I tried to push away from him, feeling the heavy weight of responsibility pressing down upon me. "I don't—I don't know if I have what it takes to kill the Jabberwocky or the Red Queen. I don't know if I'm strong enough."

"That's why I've been working with Jack and Queen Amari to make sure that you don't have to be the one to deliver the death blows."

He took a sip of wine and began to rub my back.

"I don't understand. I thought it had to be me doing it, and with me using the Vorpal Sword."

"Don't overthink it, bunny," he said, letting his fingers dance across my shoulders. I loved how his deep voice had such a soothing effect on me. It wrapped around me like a seductive caress.

"We have plans in place. And we have backup plans for them, as well as backup plans for the backup plans. We'll be fine, as long as you trust us. Have we ever let you down?"

I knew Ransom understood the gravity of the

situation, but my instincts still urged me to let him comfort me, to shield me from the darkness that loomed ahead. His presence was intoxicating, his incubus desires seeping into my thoughts, making it difficult to focus on anything else.

How could I not trust him after he'd broken into the hospital and rescued me? How could I not trust him when he'd saved me from the blue pills, or from Dinah, or from some of his worst-behaved bunnies back at the Rabbit Hole?

"No. You've never let me down. Not once."

I pulled him into a passionate kiss.

I felt a pang of guilt for enjoying this moment while the fate of our home hung in the balance, but I couldn't resist the pull of Ransom's seductive charm.

"Oh, I see how it is . . . "

Breaking the kiss, my gaze darted over to where a pair of brilliant green eyes were hovering in the air. Then Chess began to materialize around them, before slinking up to me and Ransom with a wicked grin.

"Your timing is impeccable, as always," Ransom said with a hint of chagrin.

"Yours isn't." Chess wagged a finger in his face. "You're early."

I leaned back and shot the incubus an accusatory look.

"Early? For what?"

Instead of answering right away, Ransom shared a glance with the Cheshire Cat demon, then swirled his wine in fake innocence.

"Your plan was to visit me because it might be our last chance to sleep together?"

"No."

"Yes," insisted Chess.

"Not exactly," Ransom began, his voice a balm to my frayed nerves. "Chess and I aren't here to fuck . . . we're here to help wrangle that Supreme Commander of ours and . . . "

"And help him safely drink from you while fucking you . . . " Chess added. "We thought it would help clear his mind before the final battle."

"Only if you want to," Ransom added. His gaze was steady and unwavering. "But I think you do."

I took a long sip from my glass as I mulled it over. Ransom was right. I *did* want to. Especially after that encounter at the soldiers' compound, when Jack had nailed me up against the wall while Ransom watched. I fucking *loved* that they loved to share me.

Well . . . most of them. But if Jack was going to learn how to share, this seemed like the right time to try.

"What about Callister?"

Ransom shrugged. "He offered to sit this one out. He knows Jack is . . . private."

"And Hatter?"

Chess shook his head. "Not invited. Contrary to what you might believe, we need him madder than the March Hare tomorrow."

I ran my fingertip around the rim of my wine glass, toying with the narrow edge. It was so easy to go one way or the other.

"And Jack said he's okay with this plan of yours?"

Chess let out a low laugh. "He doesn't know anything about it. But he'll do it if you ask him."

"Invite him to your room," Ransom urged in a suggestive tone. He finished his wine in one gulp and set his glass aside. Then he reached out to gently cup my chin in his hand. "Let us take your mind off things for a while. You need a distraction, bunny. Call out to Jack and tell him what you want . . . what you *need*. I'll be damned for eternity if he turns you down."

A part of me knew I should resist, that giving in to them, to this darkness, would draw me further into the shadows. But another part of me—the part that had witnessed unimaginable horrors and knew that the Red Queen must be stopped at all costs—craved the release only they could provide.

"We know you need your rest, Alice." A soft, deep purr began to rumble from Chess. His touch on my thigh was warm and soothing, his words a whispered caress. Then his feline features shifted into a mischievous smirk. "Let us put you to bed the way you deserve."

"We'll make sure you fall asleep with a smile on your face," Ransom hummed near my ear. His mouth made a trail of hot kisses down my neck as his hands roamed over my curves. They clawed gently at my breasts, teasing my nipples to hardness.

I felt a sense of calming desire settle over me. Although we were on the brink of war, in this moment, all was right with the world.

"What the hell," I breathed, succumbing to the inevitable. "You only live once, right?"

"That's right. Let us ease your burdens," Ransom murmured, his fingers tracing the curve of my jaw. "If only for tonight."

"Let us be your solace," Chess added. His fingers brushed against my arm, and he purred louder, victory gleaming in his unholy gaze. Ransom grinned, his dark eyes glinting in the moonlight streaming through my window.

"Tomorrow is going to be rough," Ransom said softly, his hand stroking through my hair. "But not as rough as Jack will be when he discovers us alone with you."

In one swift move, Chess took my wine glass just as Ransom guided me to lie back on my pillows. Everywhere his hands roamed, the fabric of my clothing disappeared, leaving me bared to them both.

The only thing on my body was Jasmine . . . my black snake tattoo from Callister. She flicked out her tongue as if to gauge the mood, then closed her eyes and grew still.

She knew I didn't need any protection from these men.

With deliberate movements, Ransom and Chess crawled onto the bed, their sinewy forms hovering over my prone body. Their hands—both human and demonic—began exploring the contours of my flesh, igniting a fire deep within me. I bit my lip, trying to suppress a moan as they stroked me with expert precision.

"Don't bite your lip, bunny," Ransom warned. "That's my job." He knelt down for a kiss while his fingers traced lazy circles over my skin.

Meanwhile, Chess's lips were pressing gentle kisses along my neck. His mouth was hot and wet against my shoulder, my ribs and hip, then my thigh, until I was squirming for him to taste me with his tentacle tongue.

I arched my back and spread my legs as arousal pooled in my core.

"No . . . " he taunted. He dragged his tongue along my outer labia, exhaling hot, warm breath on my aching pussy, yet refused to dive into it. "Not until you invite Jack to join us. Call for him, Alice."

The thought of Jack's face if he saw what these two were doing to me sent ripples of forbidden lust hammering up my spine. Goosebumps erupted all up down my arms and legs.

I wanted to make Jack jealous. I wanted him to push through the powerful hold of Chess and Ransom, and take me for his own.

I wanted him to ride me . . . claim me . . . to be so focused on getting inside of me that he didn't care who else was watching.

Jack . . . I whispered in my mind, the mental connection we shared allowing me to reach out to him. *Come to my room.*

Is everything alright? His voice echoed in my head, concern lacing his words.

Everything's fine, I assured him, glancing at

Ransom and Chess as they continued their exploration of my body. *We just...we need you here.*

Understood, Jack replied. I could sense his curiosity mixed with an unwavering sense of duty.

Ransom's lips curled into a triumphant smirk. "Good girl."

As I waited for Jack to arrive, my thoughts raced. This was a step beyond anything we'd done before—not only involving all three of them but also combining our deepest desires with the horrors that awaited us.

Yet, there was no denying the pull I felt toward each of my wicked boys of Wonderland. I needed to connect with them on a primal level before facing the darkness.

I shuddered as Ransom's fingers traced my spine, his touch igniting a fire within me. Chess's nails gently scratched my skin, lighting up my brain with the stimulation of being devoured by the two of them.

"Please . . . " I whimpered as Chess's demonic tongue stroked my inner thighs. "Why won't you fuck me?"

"Good question," Ransom sighed. He reached down to massage my clit, making his fingers vibrate and pulse. "You're so swollen and wet. You're so ready to get fucked . . . to be ridden hard." He dipped a finger inside my wetness and offered it to Chess, who licked it clean with his long, pink tongue.

"She's definitely ready for fucking," he agreed. "Where's that damned White Knight?"

The door to my room creaked open, and Jack

stepped inside, covered from neck to toe in his black leather armor. His eyes immediately locked onto the scene before him.

Ransom's fingers were buried deep inside me while Chess' mouth greedily sucked at one of my tits, sending shivers of pleasure coursing through my veins.

"Ah, Jack," Ransom murmured, pausing to address him. "So glad you could join us."

I watched his nostrils flare as he inhaled the scent of my warm, wet pussy. His gaze flicked down to my swollen, shiny pink wetness, and I knew I'd caught his attention. My clit gave a happy twitch at the sight of his pupils dilating in desire. I relaxed my knees, spreading myself, opening myself to him.

"What is this?" he asked, his voice calm and steady. But I knew that underneath that cool, calm exterior, was a bloodthirsty hunter who wanted to mount me like an animal and ride me to the edge of the world.

"Look at her," Ransom whispered in my ear, his breath hot on my skin. "She's so desperate for us, Jack. Let's show her what it means to be ours."

"Join us," Chess urged. His demon tongue slipped between my thighs, expertly caressing my clit. I gasped, my back arching as he coaxed a moan from my lips. "Alice needs to be filled in all ways, and be claimed completely."

"Jack," I shuddered beneath the sensation of four hands and two tongues simultaneously caressing nearly every inch of my body. A flush spread over my skin at the thought of adding another hard, masculine body to the mix. Jack, with his icy eyes and cool touch, was the missing piece of that puzzle. "They won't fuck me! Not until you fuck me first!"

"Take her however you want, my friend," Ransom instructed while eyeing the vampire darkly. "Fuck her. Drink her. Chess and I will make sure she's safe from your . . . *passion.*"

Jack's mouth pressed into a flat line and he tossed his long hair over his shoulder.

He looked impatient.

Annoyed as fuck.

I could hear his thoughts racing with bits and fragments here and there: *I don't have time for this . . . I should be inspecting the weapons . . . the soldiers aren't ready . . . Roxanne is almost here . . . Amari needs more time . . . there are a million things that need my attention . . .*

Suddenly his mind went silent.

I didn't hear a sound.

In that moment, there was only one thing that needed the White Knight's attention.

And we both knew what it was—

Me.

I gave a pitiful, desperate whimper to lure him closer.

Without saying a word, he walked around the bed slowly, studying me quietly. He circled me like a predator stalking its prey, his hungry eyes never leaving mine.

I swallowed hard, trembling under the weight of his gaze. "I need you," I whispered. "Please, Jack."

And all the while, Chess and Ransom kept licking me . . . teasing me . . . caressing me . . . showing me off like a prize to be had. They shamelessly played with my nipples, my tits, and delivered wet kisses along my thighs, neck, and shoulders.

"Do you want her tied up?" Ransom offered, and stopped teasing my pussy with his finger. He conjured a length of black silky rope and dragged it back and forth between my legs, making me moan from the few seconds of delicious contact it made with my clit.

Folding his arms across his chest, Jack shook his head.

He seemed almost bored by the suggestion.

"Do you want her gagged?" With a snap of his fingers, Ransom's clothes disappeared, revealing his fully erect cock. He slid his thick, veiny dick into my mouth with a satisfied hiss, plunging into the back of my throat until I was left trembling and gasping for air.

"No . . . " Jack replied, although he watched me go to town on Ransom's cock with mild interest.

One of Chess's hands transformed into a furry paw, revealing a set of long, talon-like claws where his fingernails should've been. He lightly dragged his claws from my thigh over my hip, working his way up my naked body. "Do you want her to bleed?"

A low growl rumbled in Jack's chest as his eyes widened in arousal.

"Closer . . . but no."

"Use your words, Jack," Ransom said with a sinister grin. "Tell us exactly what you want, and we will indulge your desires."

Jack narrowed his eyes and let out a breath. "Very well."

He wasn't smiling.

He was eyeing me like a white lion ready to destroy its prey.

"I want her to *run*."

CHAPTER THIRTEEN

JACK

It was all I could do not to run after Alice the moment she dashed out of the room. My desire for her swelled to a feverish pitch. I could smell her arousal, her need, everywhere. It was like ambrosia on the tainted wind.

Behind me, Ransom and Chess had shifted into their true demonic forms, all wings and horns and fangs and claws. My vampire instincts kicked in, overriding any semblance of restraint I'd struggled to maintain.

She was my prey, and tonight, I would hunt her down.

I would claim her.

She might be ours . . . but vampires hunted alone. When I found her and got inside of her, she would be *mine*.

Not 'ours.'

The twenty-second head start I'd given Alice suddenly felt like a small eternity. I listened to the clock on the wall tick, each sound ringing through my ears as her bare feet sprinted down the hall.

Even louder than the clock was the sound of her heart beating.

Faster . . .

Harder . . .

The same rhythm that I'd use to consume her once I found her.

I'd fuck her faster . . .

Drink her harder . . .

"Eighteen . . . nineteen . . . twenty," Ransom said before folding his wings behind his back.

With a growl ripped from the depths of my undead soul, I sprang into action, crashing through the bedroom door and into the moonlit hall. My preternatural senses locked onto the scent of my prey, her heartbeat like a siren's call luring me into the depths of depravity.

My predatory instincts took over as the thrill of the chase ignited a fire within me. Chess and Ransom could barely keep up as they pursued me through the dimly lit corridors of Amari's castle.

My heart pounded in my ears as I sprinted after Alice through the twisting passageways. The smell of her grew stronger with each step I took. I knew that deep down, she wanted nothing more than to be caught, to be taken, to be devoured whole.

I was closing in on her.

Not much longer, and I'd be inside her warm, wet, vibrant body.

Adrenaline coursed through my veins, making

me feel alive. This chase, this exhilarating game, was exactly what I lived for.

And no one had made me feel it so deeply until Alice had come into my world.

I followed her scent to the library and threw open the heavy wooden doors, stalking into the darkness with a gleam in my eyes.

"I know you're in here . . . " I called out to the room. Ransom shut the doors behind him and hung back with Chess.

"I can smell you . . . " I unbuckled my gauntlets and breastplate, letting them fall to the floor. I lifted my nose to the air, taking in the fragrance of dusty, ancient books, and the sweet, tangy promise of the warm gash between Alice's thighs.

My cock took notice so quickly that I barely had time to free myself from the rest of my armor. I'd considered leaving it on, yet the last thing I wanted to do was leave Wonderland's heroine chafed and raw before sending her into battle.

I prowled through the bookshelves under the pale light of the moon, shedding what garments I still wore . . . leaving a trail behind me.

I found Alice hiding behind one of a dozen tall stacks that stretched up to the ceiling. The only other barrier between us was a long, wide table.

She started to run, but her human legs were no match for my vampire speed. Driven by a primal need to claim my prize, I leapt over the table and cut her off.

She spun around and sprinted in the opposite direction.

Again, I was already standing in front of her.

My mouth spread into a grin dominated by feral hunger.

"The chase only makes your capture that much sweeter."

Wide-eyed and panting, her body was absolutely trembling with both excitement and terror. She dove under the table, shimmying between the chairs. I grabbed them and flung them across the room, oblivious to the sound of the wood splintering against the stone walls.

By the time Alice had crawled to the other side of the table, I was already there, waiting for her.

My hands curled around her warm, soft arms, holding her in an iron grip before pinning her to the top of the hard, smooth, wooden surface.

I dragged her ass to the edge of the table, pushing easily between her soft thighs, then claimed her mouth in a bruising kiss.

She moaned into my mouth, twisting her hips in a futile attempt to avoid contact with my hard length. My hands curled around her thighs, lifting her into position.

Her pulse was racing, and she was playing her part so well.

I looked deep into her wild eyes, and nearly came undone right then and there from what she whispered.

"Don't hold back."

"Never," I said out loud.

I didn't hold *anything* back.

I gave her my everything.

Alice cried out as I slid into her tight, hot, wet cunt. A grin of satisfaction spread across my face as I filled her so completely, stretching her to the limit. For a moment, I remained still, savoring the feel of our joining . . . and the feel of her back arching off the table as it yielded to me.

The tension was already coiling in my belly, tightening in my balls, ready to spring free.

Then I began to move.

My thrusts alternated between shallow and fast, to deep and slow, bringing us both to the edge of madness. She clung to me, nails scoring down my back, crying out with every plunge of my hips. I drove my cock into her relentlessly, pounding her against the unforgiving wooden surface.

The sounds of our fucking echoed through the empty library, filling it with the sounds of her moans and the slap of our flesh, wet and wanton. I hooked her leg over my arm, sinking into her at a new angle that pushed me over the edge.

Suddenly I stiffened, burying myself to the hilt as I spilled inside her with a deep, guttural groan.

"More," she begged, her eyes wide with a mixture of terror and desire. Her voice was barely audible over the pounding of my labored breathing. "I want to feel everything."

As if on cue, Ransom and Chess entered the fray. Their desire for Alice was palpable.

So was their cautious respect, their fear . . . of me.

Ignoring them, I closed my eyes and continued to fuck my prize, each powerful stroke sending shockwaves of pleasure throughout my body. Our rhythm intensified as I drove into her relentlessly, my hips rocking against hers in perfect harmony. The intensity of our coupling blurred the line between pleasure and pain, leaving my mind reeling in the carnal bliss.

The only thing that could feel better was to taste her . . .

I opened my eyes and saw Ransom looking back at me with a golden gaze.

"You don't have to stop, Jack," he said, his voice low and seductive as he approached me. His two demon cocks were standing proudly erect.

He lowered his head, and thus, his horns. I knew what he meant.

Indulge, but I will fight you if I have to.

Still fucking, I stifled a growl as the incubus maneuvered his body behind Alice's, using his flesh as a backdrop instead of the cold, hard, wooden table I'd chosen. She was panting heavily, her body glistening with sweat as she lay trembling between us.

I groaned as I sank my cock deep into her cunt, already slick from my previous release inside her. I thrusted into her with abandon, feeling her hot, wet heat envelop me. Every plunge pushed her against Ransom, who nodded in approval.

I bared my fangs at him in warning.

She was *mine.*

Mine to fuck . . . to claim.

"Jack . . . " Alice whimpered, her body trembling beneath me, locked in the throes of ecstasy. The moans that escaped her lips were music to my ears, only further fueling my passion.

"Whenever you're ready, Jack," Ransom murmured from behind her shoulder. "Drink from her. Taste her life's essence while you fuck her."

As I continued to thrust into Alice, I reveled in the feeling of her warmth surrounding me, her body pressed tightly against my own. The scent of her arousal filled my nostrils, and I knew I couldn't resist the temptation any longer. I lowered my mouth to her neck, my fangs piercing her tender flesh with ease, and drank deeply.

The warm, coppery taste of her blood filled my mouth. I allowed myself to succumb to the dark urges within me as I drank from her, while our bodies moved in perfect synchrony. The taste of her blood was intoxicating, fueling me with a primal hunger that only intensified my desire for her.

The blood bond between us let me feel Ransom's hand on her hip as he repositioned himself, teasing her puckered entrance. As much as it infuriated me, I couldn't deny the arousal it evoked, and I swallowed another mouthful of her.

"Are you ready for more, Alice?" he asked, his voice sultry and commanding.

"Yes," she panted, her body trembling with anticipation.

Ransom pushed his thick cock slowly into her ass, forcing me to pause my thrusts momentarily. I could feel the pressure of him entering her. I could hear the sound of her gasping at the invasion. It felt foreign . . . infuriating and exhilarating at the same time, having another man's shaft so close to my own, separated only by the thin barrier of her flesh.

Fighting my way through the bloodlust, I lifted my mouth off of the open wound and snarled at my competition.

"Remember your place, incubus," I growled, my eyes locked on his as I continued to fuck Alice. The sound of her moans and whimpers only spurred me on further.

"Of course, Jack," he replied smoothly. Yet a wicked grin was plastered across his face as he began to thrust into Alice's ass. His movements were slow and steady at first, but gradually increased in pace to match my own. "It's my place to ensure *both* of your pleasure. It's all about Alice, remember?"

Yes, it was all about Alice. My possessiveness warred with my arousal, but it was impossible to deny the pleasure coursing through me as I fucked her alongside Ransom under Chess's watchful gaze.

"Focus on the pleasure, Jack," Chess whispered from off to one side, his words a balm to my turbulent thoughts. "We're all here for her, to give her what she desires."

I tried to heed his advice. I bent down and latched onto the bleeding wound on her neck, concentrating on the sensations flooding my body—the feel of Alice's tight cunt wrapped around my cock, the warmth of Ransom's shaft sliding against mine through the thin barrier, and the taste of her blood filling my mouth.

My fangs sank deeper into Alice's delicate neck, the metallic taste of her blood flooding my throat as I continued to fuck her with a desperate hunger. The intensity of the moment was only heightened by Ransom's presence behind her, his thick demon cock filling her ass while I filled her cunt. It was a maddening, intoxicating blend of pleasure and jealousy.

"Let yourself go, Jack," Ransom coaxed, his voice a sultry whisper in my ear. "You and I are both creatures of the flesh. Embrace it."

I growled, my possessive instincts fighting with my desire for the pleasure we were all sharing.

Suddenly, without warning, I felt the unmistakable pressure of Ransom's second cock pushing against mine within Alice's tight, velvety walls.

"*Get out!*" I roared in his face, my eyes widening at the sensation. My jealousy raged, but it was quickly drowned out by the overwhelming pleasure that coursed through my loins.

"Give in to it, Jack," Ransom urged, his thrusts matching mine as he fucked Alice's ass, and now her pussy alongside me. "We're all here for her pleasure, after all."

As much as I wanted to pull Ransom off her by his wings and throw him against the wall, the truth was impossible to ignore—this felt fucking incredible. I'd never experienced anything so intensely erotic before, our cocks sliding together inside her slick, quivering core.

"Fuck," Ransom groaned, his voice strained with lust and exertion as our cocks slid in and out of Alice's tight, velvety sex in perfect harmony. "You feel that? She's taking both of us so well."

"Ransom," Alice moaned, her eyes squeezed shut as she surrendered herself completely to the overwhelming sensations coursing through her body. "Jack . . . don't stop."

I gritted my teeth at the thought of sharing such an intimate moment with another man, but with every satisfied sigh and moan Alice let out, my resolve crumbled. The way his wet, sticky balls brushed and pressed against mine as we fucked the same cunt only served to fan the flames of my desire.

"Tell us, bunny . . . do you like having us fill your holes?"

"Yeah . . . I mean, yes, my king," Alice whispered, her voice soft and breathless as she gazed up at me with wide, adoring eyes. "My White Knight . . . "

I could feel our combined efforts sending waves of ecstasy coursing through her body. Every whimper, every gasp from her lips only served to fuel our carnal lust.

But when Alice had looked up at me and called me her White Knight, I forgot all about that other man. I had only one response . . . one duty.

"Come for me, my queen."

I dipped my head down to her neck, licking the trickles of blood before settling my mouth over her one last time. Then I reached down to rub the swollen bud between her legs with practiced skill.

Alice immediately trembled from the force of her impending climax. Despite my initial reservations, the sensation of Ransom's cock against mine was undeniably exquisite.

"I can feel her getting close . . . can't you?" he murmured.

I blinked in agreement as I swallowed another mouthful of delicious blood. My own climax was on the horizon.

"Do it, Jack. Make her come for us," said Chess, who was clearly enjoying the spectacle.

"Come on, bunny," Ransom coaxed. "Show us how much you love having two cocks buried inside you."

"Jack . . . Ransom . . . " Alice panted, her body beginning to tremble as her orgasm built within her. "Oh god . . . I'm gonna . . . "

"Yes . . . that's it. Let it out," he urged. I growled in approval, the taste of her blood so rich on my tongue as I drove into her with renewed vigor. "Show us what you're made of."

With a final, skillful flick of my slick fingers, Alice screamed, her orgasm washing over her like a tidal wave, drenching my belly in the process. Warm, wet fluid gushed down my abdomen as more warm, wet fluid gushed down my throat.

The pulsing contractions of her sopping wet cunt milked both Ransom and me. My breath hitched as I struggled not to spill inside her.

Not yet.

Not until that incubus did first.

Alice cried out again, her wails echoing through the library, her hands clutching at me as I slammed into her. Ransom squeezed her breasts from behind, pinching her nipples. I could feel his hard length pressing against mine, separated only by the thin wall of her flesh. The sensation drove me wild, my thrusts becoming brutal and erratic.

The taste of her blood and the feel of Ransom's balls smashed against mine sent wave after wave of ecstasy crashing through me, more intense than anything I'd experienced before.

"Fuck!" Ransom bellowed, his own orgasm overtaking him as he coated the walls of Alice's pussy with his liquid heat.

With a guttural roar, I surrendered to the overwhelming pleasure, my cock pulsing inside Alice as I unleashed my seed deep within her once more. I could feel Ransom doing the same, his own orgasm ripping through him as he filled her ass and her cunt with his hot, sticky essence. Our seed mixed within her, filling her completely as we all reveled in the sinful pleasure of our shared release.

The second my climax began to subside, Chess pulled my mouth from Alice's neck with two massive paws and a growl of warning. I stared at the trickle of crimson that marred Alice's flawless skin, hunger still gnawing at me.

"Enough now, Jack," Chess warned while narrowing his eyes. "You know how easy it is to lose control."

"I *do* know," I muttered, my body still twitching with aftershocks of pleasure.

Breathless, I withdrew from Alice's cunt. My body felt so alive that it wasn't merely buzzing . . . it was trembling. My gaze met Ransom's, and despite the conflict within me, a new understanding passed between us.

Alice belonged to *all* of us, in body and blood, and we would share her as we had shared this moment.

Not always, but a future where we shared her like this was possible.

The bitter taste of jealousy mixed with desire lingered on my tongue as I gazed down at my queen, who lay panting beneath me, using Ransom as a pillow. Her body was slick with sweat and cum.

"Look at what we did to her, Jack," Ransom purred, his voice dripping with satisfaction. "She took us both, and she loved it. Admit it—you loved it as well."

Unable to help the possessiveness that surged within me, I could only growl in response. While I couldn't deny the carnal thrill I'd experienced feeling a sex demon inside Alice alongside me, admitting that truth out loud tasted like ash in my mouth.

"Jack," Alice whispered breathlessly, her fingers tracing the contours of my face. "That was fucking incredible. I hope we live long enough to do that again."

"I do, too," I replied without much thought.

As we disentangled ourselves and began cleaning

up the evidence of our debauchery, I couldn't shake the growing doubt that lurked in the darkest recesses of my mind, whispering about the possibility of loss and heartbreak.

'I hope we live long enough to do that again . . .'

It was such a staggering comment from such an unassuming mouth.

I stared out the moonlit window, my thoughts swirling like a tempestuous storm, pulling me under its dark embrace.

Images of blood and carnage flashed before my eyes, the very air around me becoming suffocating and heavy. The weight of the looming battle against the Red Queen and her army bore down on me, threatening to crush me beneath its merciless heel.

My heart was heavy with concern for my new hunting companions, who'd not only indulged my wishes, but managed to push me out of my comfort zone for the first time in hundreds of years. My heart ached with tenderness and affection for the human in our midst, who had just conjured a warm outfit to keep the frosty air off her beautiful body.

A spark of orange caught my eye, and I peered out the window once more. It looked like a torch.

"Chess? My soldiers know better than to give away their location. Can you go see who that is?"

I pointed to the tiny speck of light just as he floated over to me.

"I'll be right back."

He disappeared into the ether as I continued to

stare out the window. Alice and Ransom sidled up to me.

"What's wrong?"

"Someone's out there with a torch," I said quietly.

"I don't see anything."

"You wouldn't," Ransom told Alice. "Not with your human eyes. But there is absolutely someone out there. Look, Jack. There's another one."

Cool air prickled at the back of my neck as I impatiently waited for the Cheshire Cat's return. The meadow between Amari's castle and the forest stretched before us, empty for now. But in the distance, a dark smudge marred the horizon.

When Chess reappeared, the look on his face told me exactly what I feared.

"It's time," he said with a somber expression. "The Red Queen is here."

CHAPTER
FOURTEEN

ALICE

The cold air bit at my exposed skin as we entered the war room of Amari's castle. I couldn't shake the feeling of dread that enveloped me, but I had to remain focused. Chess and Ransom flanked me, their faces etched with determination. In front of us, Jack, Amari, Winston, Callister, and Hatter were huddled over the map and figurines positioned around the large table, discussing battle strategies.

"Alright, everyone," Amari said, her voice carrying an authoritative tone that demanded attention. "The plan is set. The Red Queen's army will be here within the hour."

"What's the plan?" I asked.

"We're going to use you as bait," Jack replied, locking his deadly red gaze on mine. The thought terrified me, but I knew I needed to do whatever it took to help save Wonderland. "You'll walk onto the snowy field with Ransom and Callister and wave a white flag of surrender to the Red Army."

My mouth went dry at the thought of walking into that big empty field, defenseless and alone.

"*That's* the plan?" I hissed. "You want me to *surrender*?"

"Yes."

Callister lit a cigarette and stepped forward, craning his neck to peer at the map. A strand of bright teal hair fell from his pompadour and into his handsome, tattooed face.

Jack leaned past him and pointed to a flat area with no coverage from the White Army. "You and Ransom will accompany Alice to this location. Then wait for the signal."

"Right," Callister acknowledged with a nod.

Flabbergasted, I put my hands on my hips. Jack was the White Knight—the best warrior in Wonderland. He was the Supreme Commander of Amari's army. This plan made no sense.

"Are you *insane*? After all we've been through, you want me to go out there and surrender to that heinous bitch?"

"Yes." He lifted a brow as if warning me not to question him further.

"Alice, it's okay," Callister said in between purple puffs of a blueberry-scented cigarette. "You won't be alone."

"Trust us," Jack reassured me with a sly grin. "Ransom and Callister will be with you every step of the way, ensuring your safety."

I swallowed hard and lifted my chin, trying to act more confident than I felt. "Fine."

Even though I was nervous as fuck, I knew better than to keep arguing about it. Clearly Jack had some kind of trick up his sleeve. Waving a white flag *did* sound a lot easier than going berserk against Roxanne with the Vorpal Sword.

But surrendering sounded unacceptable.

Jack's eyes softened as he regarded me. "I know what I'm doing, Alice. I won't let any harm come to you. You have my word."

Amari nodded, her expression grim. "It's a solid plan. Let's end this war tonight, and take back our kingdom at long last."

As I stood there, my mind raced with a thousand different scenarios. How were we supposed to take back the kingdom if we were surrendering? How could I carry out the plan if I didn't know the overall strategy? What if the plan went wrong? What if Ransom and Callister couldn't save me? What if the Jabberwocky came out of nowhere and killed us? We were sitting ducks out there.

But I pushed those thoughts aside, focusing on the task at hand.

"Everyone, get to your positions," Jack ordered. "Time is running out."

As we left the war room and split off in different directions, I tried to quell the pounding in my chest. I had to trust Jack and Amari. I had to trust Ransom and Callister.

More importantly, I had to trust myself. Everyone was depending on me, and I wouldn't let them down.

With the plan set in motion, I soon found myself trudging towards the center of a massive, barren field. My breath made clouds of warm fog in the icy air. The thick, heavy snow crunched under my boots as I forced one foot in front of the other.

To my right and left were Ransom and Callister. In my arms was a huge white flag. The cold wind rippled the white fabric, making it billow out and snap hard against the dark backdrop of the moonlit night sky.

The bitter wind sliced through my clothes as we surveyed the vast, flat, empty field. I'd been told not to overdress, and now I was freezing my ass off. I felt so exposed and vulnerable out here, with nothing to protect me except an incubus and a caterpillar shifter. Jack had insisted that I leave my armor and my weapon back at the castle, although he refused to tell me the reason why.

In the distance, a sea of darkness consumed the horizon, waiting to unleash Roxanne's Red Army upon us. I knew they were out there, arrows knocked and swords drawn. I squinted through the darkness, searching for more torches, or even the glint of steel reflecting the moonlight.

There was nothing.

But I knew we weren't alone.

My heart pounded against my chest, threatening to burst through my ribcage. Other than my heavy breathing, it was all I could hear in the unsettling quiet. My stomach churned with anticipation and dread.

The air was heavy with the scent of impending battle, and the tension between us was palpable. Roxanne, our nemesis, was nowhere to be seen, but her presence loomed over us like a dark cloud.

I could feel her out there in the darkness.

Lurking.

Watching.

Waiting.

"Wave the flag again," said Ransom. "I can see movement in the trees."

"I hope you guys know what you're doing," I muttered, still waving the flag against the cold wind.

"Of course we do," Ransom assured me, although his gaze was pinned on the horizon. His breath was visible in the frigid air. "We won't let anything happen to you."

Callister remained silent, but I could sense his hyper-vigilance. He kept turning in tight circles, scanning the edge of the field for any signs of movement.

"They're in position. Just like we expected."

"Good," Ransom said before glancing at me. "Ready?"

"Can you give me five minutes?" I joked, hoping to ease the tension. He shook his head and offered me a weak smile.

"Not likely. Here they come," he murmured, his eyes narrowing on the distant figures as they marched toward us through the snow. I could feel the tension radiating off him in waves. All it did was manage to heighten my own anxiety.

"Hold steady. Don't move until I give the order."

My eyes widened as I got a better look at the first wave of Roxanne's soldiers emerging from the darkness. Their black uniforms were a stark contrast against the white moonlit snow. They streamed onto the edges of the field, their numbers growing by the second.

"Uhhh . . . how long until you give that order?" I asked with a shaky voice. "Now seems like a really good time to bail."

"We have to wait for the signal," he replied through a set jaw.

"What's the signal?"

"You'll know it when you see it."

In the near distance, shouts rang out. The sound of clanging armor and marching boots followed, growing louder and louder. More and more of the black-armored figures emerged from the woods around the field, weapons glinting under the pale moon.

"Hold your position," Ransom said beside me. I could see the black angular shape of his demon wings start to rise out of his back.

Tiny moving orbs of fire caught my attention, and I turned back to face the Red Army.

My breath caught in my throat at the sight of them spread all around the horizon.

Fuck!

They had us completely surrounded! There were so many of them, an endless wave of soldiers pouring into the field from every direction. My stomach twisted into knots at the sight, and I started to panic.

"Steady," Callister said in a calm voice, although he was gripping my arm tightly.

"Easy for you to say." It was impossible not to feel afraid when faced with such overwhelming odds. Thousands of soldiers marched towards us in perfect formation.

But Jack wouldn't have sent me out here to die. And if Callister and Ransom weren't afraid, then I shouldn't be, either.

I did as I was told.

I stood firm, clutching my flag and waiting. It felt so wrong to be standing perfectly still while we were being charged at full speed. I sighed and shifted my weight from one foot to the other as we waited. The anticipation was suffocating, and I found myself longing to run . . . but there was nowhere to go. Not when there were soldiers bearing down on us from every direction.

Beside me, Ransom shifted anxiously. Still waving my flag, I looked up at him. "How much longer until we see that signal?"

His lips curled into a predatory smile. "Soon. Not yet, but soon."

"I'm not letting go of you, Alice," Callister assured me, his voice soft and comforting. I glanced at him, grateful for his presence.

Inhaling deeply, I steeled myself as the soldiers drew nearer, their footsteps crunching in the snow. They were so fucking close. Their swords were raised . . . their arrows were aimed at us and ready to fly. My heart pounded as I braced myself, hoping against hope that Jack and Amari's insane plan to have me surrender had better pay off.

Like, *soon*.

Really fucking soon.

"Wait for it," Ransom instructed, his voice low and urgent. The sound of arrows flying at us pierced the air, and my heart leapt into my throat. All I wanted to do was run.

Suddenly a loud boom thundered across the sky, making a sound like ripping fabric. I looked up to see a giant fireball hurtling towards us.

"That's the signal!" Ransom shouted at me. "Drop the flag!"

Stunned, I froze in place.

All I could do was watch the fireball coming towards us while his black demon horns grew from his head. In a rage, he grabbed the flag out of my hands and hurled it like a javelin at the approaching soldiers.

Another round of arrows began to fly at us. One landed in the snow only a few feet from my boots. Before I could scream or try again to run, enormous green and blue wings burst from Callister's back. He snatched me into his powerful arms with lightning-fast reflexes and soared upward, dodging arrows as he carried me off into the sky.

Beneath us, Ransom let out a furious roar and pushed a circular shockwave of magic at the soldiers. It shook the ground hard enough to make most of them stumble and fall over. Then he outstretched his black demon wings and shot up into the darkness.

From the safety of Callister's arms, I stared at the giant fireball in the sky. Flames rolled off the back of it as it made a graceful arc, then began to fall down . . . down . . . down . . .

"Shields up!" one soldier bellowed in a desperate attempt to save his comrades. But it was futile.

The fireball smashed into the ground where he and at least twenty soldiers had been standing just a few seconds ago, leaving a huge black hole.

The soldiers' faces contorted with horror as they realized the deadly trap they'd marched directly into.

It took me a bit longer to understand.

More cannons hidden in the surrounding landscape roared to life. Flaming balls of iron ripped through the air, smashing into the soldiers on the field.

As Callister carried me higher into the sky, the frigid wind was freezing my face off, but I didn't care. Mesmerized, I stared at the horrific, awesome scene unfolding below me.

A relentless shower of fireballs shot towards the soldiers from the darkness, shattering the field like glass. They fell into the darkness, screaming as the land gave way to black nothingness. There wasn't even any fire. It was almost as if there was nothing there to burn.

"What's happening to the field?" I yelled at Callister through the wind.

"It's not a field," he replied with a sinister laugh. "We lured them onto a lake!"

"A *lake*? Holy shit!" My jaw fell as I watched more fiery cannonballs blast away the ice beneath the Red Army's feet. The ice hidden beneath the snow began to crack even more. The sound echoed across the desolate field like a thousand breaking bones. Clusters of soldiers disappeared from sight by the dozens.

Holding me close, he pumped his wings and turned to get a better view. Fireballs lit up the night sky so brightly that I had a perfect view of the Red Queen's soldiers being obliterated in groups of fifty or more.

They thrashed in the icy water, scrambling onto floating bodies or chunks of ice, only to be hit by another blast of a flaming cannonball. After the torture and terror they'd put me and Callister through, I had no sympathy for them. I'd rather be dead than serve the Red Queen.

"Nice work, bunny." I turned in the direction of the familiar voice, and saw Ransom flying beside us. The wicked smile on his face was priceless. "You've just put a massive dent in Roxanne's forces."

Callister easily navigated away from the chaos, depositing me in the courtyard of the fortress outside Amari's castle. I landed on shaking legs, my pulse racing with shock and wonder at the carnage I'd just witnessed.

Multiple fires were blazing in designated areas, and I hobbled over to the nearest one to warm my frozen face and hands. I felt a cold slithering sensation on my upper right arm and was surprised to see Jasmine, my living snake tattoo, poke her little black head out of my sleeve.

"I forgot you're cold-blooded. You must be freezing," I said, stepping closer to the heat. She flicked out her black cobra tongue and shifted her body until every inch of her was the same temperature as my skin. Once she'd warmed up, she slithered back onto my skin, content to exist in two dimensions instead of three.

I imagined myself in toasty base layers, protected by the exquisite armor that I'd worn during my more advanced sword training sessions. The magic worked easily enough, but when I tried to conjure the Vorpal Sword, it was useless.

I glanced around, taking in the flurry of activity as soldiers from the White Army prepared for the next phase of the battle. Judging by the urgency around me, Roxanne would be here soon.

Through the crackling orange flames, I saw Jack speaking to one of his officers. He had a sword hanging on each side of his hips, and his horned helmet was tucked securely under one arm. The two of them were close enough for me to overhear them speak.

"Do you have any reports from the front line?"

"Yes, Commander. We've decimated over seventy percent of the Red Queen's soldiers without losing a single one of ours. Not one! You couldn't have had a better outcome. If you see

Alice, tell her the troops appreciate her cooperation."

"I will see her, and I will tell her," Jack nodded. I felt a sudden rush of pride shoot through me to know the full vision of his plan. It was brilliant.

It was also twisted as fuck—luring them onto a frozen lake under the guise of surrender, then bombing the shit out of them—but I loved knowing what my Jack of Diamonds was capable of.

He was a lot like the King of Clubs.

He didn't play fair.

Jack played to win.

Only this wasn't a game. This was life or death. This was the fate of Wonderland.

He caught my gaze through the fire and dismissed the officer. Then he immediately strode towards me. He stopped in front of me, his eyes roaming over my armor as a fierce grin split his beautiful face.

"I'd say we've eliminated at least seventy percent of the Red Army, thanks to you. Well done, Alice."

Heat rose in my cheeks. "I just did what I was told."

"You did more than that." Jack reached out, cupping my face in his free hand. "You trusted me with your life. Everything about that plan depended on you being part of it. If anyone else had gone to the lake with a white flag, Roxanne would've instantly known it was a trap."

My heart skipped a beat at his praise, at his touch, and at the warmth in his eyes. Before I could respond, he dipped his head and pressed his mouth against mine.

The kiss was searing, full of passion and urgency. I melted into it, my hands coming up to grip his shoulders. We broke apart, breathless, and for a long moment just stared at each other.

I don't want this to be the end . . .

Neither do I . . .

Then how do we stop this?

"We don't stop it," he said out loud. "We fight. We fight as hard and as smart as we can. And we remember that we aren't alone in this fight."

I nodded, trying to ignore the lingering tingle on my lips. I didn't want to be the first one of us to let go. Finally, he took a deep breath and stepped back, taking in the sight of my wicked boys, Queen Amari, and all of our troops preparing for the imminent final battle.

"What do I do now?"

He snickered to himself as he handed me his helmet. I watched as he unbuckled one of the swords from his hips and fastened it around my waist. I instantly recognized the gleaming blade imbued with ancient magic and deadly potential.

"Take the Vorpal Sword. Kill the bad guys. Bonus points for taking out the Jabberwocky and the Red Queen."

His blood-red eyes pinned onto mine, filled with a mix of concern and determination. We both knew that he couldn't teach me any more. I'd learned and practiced and studied as much as I could.

This was the moment it had all boiled down to.

"Thank you," I said, trying not to cry. I found myself shivering from more than just the cold. "Thank you for everything, Jack. I'll try not to let you down."

"Remember your training," he said, keeping his tone firm. It felt as if it were both a promise and a farewell. Then, he conjured a helmet and placed it on my head before taking back his own horned one.

The second he slipped it on his head, he transformed into an ominous devil. His two long horns curved and rose above his head, making him look more like a demon than a former human-turned-vampire.

The two narrow slits over his eyes glowed red with foreboding. They hid whatever softness was in them, replacing Jack with a terrifying monster only known as the White Knight.

"Are you ready?" he asked, his voice a blend of authority and tenderness.

I nodded, swallowing hard.

"Ready as I'll ever be," I answered, my heart pounding in anticipation. My grip tightened around the hilt of my sword while I mentally prepared myself for the confrontation ahead. I could hear the Red Army swarming outside the fortress. The White Army was doing all they could to fight them off, but their bloodlust was evident in their frenzied battle cries.

The fortress gates groaned as they were assaulted with battering rams, and then hacked away with axes.

Chaos erupted as wood splintered and the Red Queen's soldiers stormed through the gate with ferocity like I'd never seen before. They spilled into the fort like a mudslide, leaving a trail of bodies and bloodstained snow behind them.

"Everyone is here to help you!" Jack shouted at me over the cacophony. "You're not alone in this, Alice!"

I gave him a brave smile, even though the air crackled with tension and a palpable sense of impending doom. With no more moves to make, I drew the Vorpal Sword from its sheath and followed him into the fray.

Everywhere I looked was a spectacular display of violence and gore. The White Army easily seemed to outnumber the Red Army and met them head-on, clashing steel against steel, magic against magic.

I watched as Jack swiftly cut through enemy soldiers, never even pausing as their blood splattered his gleaming white armor.

On the other end of the fort, Amari used her magic to strike down her enemies, sending purple bolts of electricity from her fingertips.

Ransom and Callister took to the sky, their crossbows in hand. Their arrows flew straight and true, piercing Red Army soldiers with deadly accuracy.

Below them, Chess shifted into his giant Cheshire Cat demon form, his body a terrifying mass of muscle and teeth. He made quick work of any soldier stupid enough to attack him. His semi-transparent form made him near impossible to hit.

And then there was Hatter. His unique madness had manifested as powerful bursts of magic that wreaked havoc on the battlefield. In a chaotic dance of destruction, his wild gestures sent shockwaves of energy that tossed soldiers aside like rag dolls or made their weapons shatter in their hands.

At least a few times, their heads simply exploded.

I made sure to stay out of his way.

As my heart raced, I focused on my training, relying on my instincts to guide me. At first I thought I could get away with only defending myself, but not when soldiers were coming at me from multiple directions.

The Vorpal Sword cut through flesh and bone like it was warm butter. Each body was a grim necessity in this brutal war. Even though I was terrified, I couldn't afford to hesitate.

Not when the fate of Wonderland hung in the balance.

"Stay sharp, Alice!" Chess called out between vicious bites, his eyes wild with bloodlust. "We're counting on you!"

Blowing a stray strand of hair out of my face, I steeled myself, pushing past the horror of it all and fighting for my friends, my lovers, my chosen family. The taste of iron mingled with the bitter cold of the night air, a twisted reminder of the bloody battle taking place around me.

"They're breaching the south wall!" Ransom bellowed from the sky above us, pointing at the vulnerable location of the fortress. One large group of our soldiers broke off to stop the invasion, their swords and magic cutting through the enemy like a merciless storm.

The screams of the dying and the clashing of weapons filled my ears as we fought on, each step forward bringing us closer to victory or death. The coppery scent of blood and gore hung heavy in the air. Steam rose from the fresh corpses littering the courtyard. And even though I didn't have a fucking clue what fate awaited me, I'd never felt more alive.

"Push them back!" Jack ordered, his voice carrying over the chaos. I watched in awe as he cut down enemy after enemy, a whirlwind of silver and determination. My heart swelled with gratitude and pride for the man who had taught me so much.

"Stay close to Alice and Amari!" Callister shouted to the soldiers.

I gripped the hilt of the Vorpal Sword tightly, my knuckles turning white with the effort. In the heat of battle, I stopped overthinking and relied on the training Jack had given me. My movements were becoming second nature as I fought against the Red Queen's soldiers.

My first kill came faster than I'd expected. A soldier lunged at me, his sword raised high. Panic surged through me, but my instincts kicked in. I sidestepped his attack before driving my blade through his chest.

Blood spurted from the wound, painting the dirty snow a deep shade of crimson. I wrenched the sword free as my heart thumped wildly at what I'd just done, but there was no time for full-blown remorse.

"Not bad," I whispered to myself, as if setting a morbid goal would make the killing easier to deal with.

I kept fighting, each swing of my sword fueled by adrenaline and terror. My second kill was messier—my blade cleaved through the chick's midsection, spilling her entrails onto the ground in a slimy, pink display. The putrid stench of half-digested food hit me hard.

"Eww! Fucking *gross*!"

Everything became a blur of motion, yet strangely, the panic went away and I settled into a strange groove. I didn't have to think about what to do—I already knew where to put my feet, how to hold my sword. All I had to do was kill the bad guys, just like Jack said.

Slash.

Lunge.

Parry.

Kill.

Repeat.

With every attack, my body began to move without thinking. My mind adapted to the carnage around me. I swung my sword and a soldier's head rolled away from his lifeless body, his eyes still wide with shock. A soldier's neck opened beneath my blade, unleashing a thick spurt of blood that sprayed across my face.

As the battle raged on, the Red Queen's forces

pressed forward, her dark magic fueling their relentless advance. Amari's soldiers fought valiantly, but they struggled to hold their ground against the onslaught. It was clear that Roxanne had grown stronger, her evil seeping into every corner of the battlefield like a poisonous fog.

"Save your strength!" Amari commanded as she dodged a bright neon blue stream of magic. "The worst of it is yet to come!"

Panting, sweating, I gripped my sword and prepared for the next attack. But something about that particular shade of neon blue triggered me, and my eyes darted over to the source of the light.

Dinah.

That fucking bitch.

And what a coward, to not bother showing up until now . . . *after* the Red Queen's army had done most of the work.

As much as I wanted to lunge for her face and rip it off, there was something about her delayed arrival that gave me pause.

Why *had* she waited until now to show up?

And where the hell was Roxanne?

Maybe more importantly . . . where was the Jabberwocky?

Flames licked up all around the outer walls of the fort, sending black smoke billowing into the sky. It was so thick that I couldn't see the moon. I could hardly see Callister or Ransom, and they weren't that high up above me.

The sky was as clear as mud. The smoky air was

getting harder to breathe. I knew that we were running out of time. And as my gaze met Amari's across the fighting soldiers and the dead bodies littering the courtyard, I could see the same fear reflected in her eyes.

I suddenly remembered the threat Dinah had made the last time I saw her.

She told me that Wonderland would burn.

But I would be damned if the Red Queen was going to rule over the ashes.

It was time to take these bitches down.

CHAPTER FIFTEEN

ALICE

The chaos inside the castle courtyard was overwhelming. Screams and shouts filled the air as swords clashed and magic crackled. The last traces of snow were gone, replaced with bloodstained mud and gravel. Pools of crimson bled out from beneath the bodies strewn across my field of vision.

Arrows flew like rain, swords clashed, and spells filled the air like fireworks. Bodies dropped like dominos, and the snow turned crimson. Ransom and Callister were in their element, fighting off assailants left and right, their supernatural strength and speed on full display as their crossbows rained arrows down on Roxanne's soldiers.

An explosion of multicolored light revealed Hatter using the full force of his magic. Confusion and madness spread through the ranks of our enemies, making some of them turn on each other in their altered state.

My heart raced in my chest, adrenaline pumping

through my veins as I watched the carnage unfolding in front of me.

"Save your strength!" Amari repeated as she leapt towards me and deflected another blue stream of Dinah's magic. "The Red Queen is here!"

The ground shook beneath my feet as the stones from the south wall gave way and collapsed. Dust and smoke and fire swirled around the gaping hole as more soldiers poured through it.

"Amari! Watch out!" I yelled, pushing her out of the way as a bolt of red lightning shot toward us. We both rolled to safety, narrowly avoiding the deadly attack. I glanced up, my breath catching in my throat as I saw the source of the spell.

A towering, gaunt figure emerged from the smoke and fire, her crimson armor like a statue made of blood.

There she stood . . . the Red Queen, in all her twisted glory.

As she stepped over the rubble, the bulging veins and pustules on her face throbbed like they were about to burst. Her neck was covered with so many infected sores that I barely noticed the string of small rubies encircling it.

Her eyes glowed with the greed of a power-hungry megalomaniac, and her lips twisted into a cruel, yellow smile. "So, sister, we finally meet on the battlefield," she sneered at Amari.

"Roxanne, this has to end!" Amari shouted back, desperation lacing her voice. "You've caused enough pain and suffering!"

"Enough? There is no such thing as enough!" Roxanne threw back her head and laughed, her voice chillingly cold. Her red, scabbed lips curled into a smug smile as she stepped forward in a leisurely walk. "Wonderland is already mine. Stop getting in my way!"

She flung a red lightning bolt at Amari, who immediately countered it with a bright purple one. The two colors clashed mid-air, crackling and shooting out sparks. I hit the ground, ducking just in time to avoid another blue blast from Dinah.

Slowly, Amari was gaining position, advancing steadily towards the Red Queen. She reached into her breastplate and pulled out the white velvet pouch, which was glowing with warm, rosy red light. Using one hand to maintain her magic, Amari curled her fingers around the pouch that held the majority of the Heart of Wonderland.

As the two sisters locked gazes, the small rubies on Roxanne's necklace seemed to vibrate with anticipation around her neck. They started to glow like they were alive, then lifted up and began reaching toward Amari with a magnetic pull. Their deep red glow intensified as they were drawn toward the pouch in Amari's hand.

The glowing stones began to strain harder and harder against their settings, stretching and twisting the metal until they finally broke free with a quick round of brittle snaps. The ruby fragments streaked across the space between the two queens, then instantly fused with the Heart of Wonderland in a fiery flash of dark pink.

The air around us vibrated and hummed with electricity and tension. I watched the white velvet pouch as it burned away in Amari's hand to reveal the Heart of Wonderland in its fully restored grandeur. The battlefield fell into an eerie silence as a blinding red light shot out of the Heart, forcing everyone to shield their eyes.

For a moment, all was still. The two armies froze in place, stunned into silence by the incredible display of the purest magical power in all of Wonderland. The light was so bright, so intense, that I could feel it in my ears . . . in my brain.

Then I felt a hum of electricity warming my chest. I stopped panting, and my aching muscles no longer burned from overexertion. I realized that Amari was using the Heart to restore the health and strength of everyone in her army.

"NO!" Roxanne screamed, realizing she'd been stripped of her greatest source of power. Her desperate shrieks cut through the thick smoke and fire that swirled around us all. The second the light began to fade, I opened my eyes to see the Red Queen's hideous face contorted with rage.

She lunged at Amari, her pitiful, weakened magic sputtering as she tried to steal back the now-whole Heart. I laughed as the desperation crept into her voice.

The tide had turned against her.

Some of her soldiers had already surrendered and

laid down their weapons. I was debating whether or not to sheath the Vorpal Sword when a streak of blue light caught my eye.

"Amari!" I cried out, my heart pounding in my chest as I darted in front of her. I watched as a neon blue dagger barreled right at me. It sliced through my armor, cutting my left shoulder as I dove in front of my queen. I cried out at the explosion of pain, dropping to my knees as my vision went white, then hit the ground hard.

Through the haze of my agony, I heard Dinah's terrified shriek.

I looked up from the cold mud just in time to watch Chess pounce on her in his bloody beast form and maul her to death. Even though I'd wanted to rip her face off earlier, once Chess did it for me, I knew there was no way in hell that I could ever do anything so horrific.

Rolling over, I dragged myself over to where Amari lay sprawled on the ground.

"Alice . . . " she said weakly, staring up at me in shock. At first I thought she was only stunned, and most likely had the wind knocked out of her. But I could tell it was serious by the excruciating pain etched across her face. I glanced down and saw a hole in her chest big enough for me to fit my fist in.

My shoulders sank.

She was fucked.

"We can fix this," I panted as White Army soldiers closed ranks around us, temporarily shielding us from harm. "You're a healer. We can fix this!"

Channeling all my medical knowledge from watching reruns of Grey's Anatomy, I sliced off part of her clothing with my sword, stuffing the cleanest part into the wound to stop the bleeding. Ignoring the searing pain in my left shoulder, I applied pressure. Then I waited for a hot surgeon with perfect hair and gorgeous eyes to take charge.

"Alice . . . " she whispered. Knowing that she was circling the drain, I lowered my head close to hers, ready to listen to her last words. "My sister is dead. Kill whatever is left of her . . . Do it for me . . . for Wonder . . . land . . . "

Then the White Queen's eyes rolled into the back of her head and her body went limp.

I looked up just in time to see Ransom swoop down and land only inches from us. Without hesitation, without a single word, he scooped up Amari's lifeless body into his arms and soared away from the battle. My heart threatened to shatter as I watched them disappear into the smoky night air, but I couldn't let myself fall apart now.

The White Queen was dead, and now the Heart of Wonderland was missing.

I whipped around just as a blast of red magic struck the row of soldiers who had been standing between their injured queen and Roxanne. They fell where they stood, their flesh withering and bones crumbling to dust inside their armor. A scream caught in my throat at the sight of the Heart of Wonderland firmly clenched in the Red Queen's hands.

The boils and scabs on her face had completely disappeared, making her so beautiful that I could hardly look away from her.

Triumph lit her face as she turned the Heart over in her hands. "At last . . . All the power of Wonderland is in my hands, and it's all mine to control . . . "

My eyes darted around in search of my wicked boys. I saw Jack battling against half a dozen soldiers just by himself. With a simple motion of her hands, Roxanne ordered her army to keep me isolated.

Her eyes narrowed on me, the only one still standing between her and victory. "Now it's just the two of us, Alice. But as you've surely noticed, there's only room for one queen of Wonderland. Once you're dead, no one will be left to challenge me."

Fury bubbled within me, hot and searing, threatening to consume everything in its path. I needed to avenge Amari and reclaim the Heart of Wonderland before Roxanne could use its power to destroy us all.

Forgetting about my injured left shoulder, I almost lost my balance, slipping in the red mud beneath my boots.

"You vicious bitch!" I snarled as I pulled myself to my feet. "You'll pay for what you've done!"

"No, I won't," she sneered, her eyes filled with malicious delight. "But I'd love to see you try and make me."

With a clumsy move, I sidestepped the Red Queen's next attack. Her blast of magic sliced through the air where I'd been standing only seconds earlier. I could feel the power of the Heart of

Wonderland as it pulsed in the cage of her fingers, almost as if it was calling out to be rescued.

"What's the matter, Roxanne?" I taunted, flashing my weapon. "Don't you know how to fight with a sword?"

The beautiful, evil queen scoffed at my challenge. "As if you could stop me." She slipped the Heart of Wonderland into her armor, then withdrew her sword. Ruby red magic crackled at its tip.

Ignoring the chaos all around me, I charged towards her, my Vorpal Sword gleaming in the faint firelight. I drew on every ounce of strength and cunning I'd learned from Jack during our training sessions.

Roxanne and I clashed, our swords sparking with red magical energy as they met. The sound of metal striking metal rang through the air, accompanied by our ragged breaths. Although we weren't evenly matched, I knew I couldn't falter—not now, when so much was at stake.

"Pathetic!" she hissed, her sword slicing through the air mere inches from my face. "You think you can avenge your precious White Queen? You think you have the skill to take Wonderland for yourself? You're nothing but a foolish girl playing at heroics."

"Shut up!" I spat, parrying her attack and countering with a swift thrust of my own. Roxanne deflected it easily, her laughter ringing in my ears. I conjured a steaming hot pumpkin spice latte and threw it in her face. The scalding hot liquid only seemed to fuel her strength.

"Ah, so much fire," Roxanne taunted, her blade meeting mine with equal fervor. "And yet, you're still so very weak. Why don't you admit that you're out of your depth?"

Ignoring her words, I channeled my anger into determination. I did the same with the painful ache in my shoulder. The sticky warmth of the blood was soaked into my sleeve, but it only made my resolve harden like ice.

"Give up, Alice," Roxanne said, her voice dripping with malice. "You'll never win. Not when I have the Heart of Wonderland in my possession."

"Never," I hissed, my determination unwavering.

I dodged and weaved, avoiding her attacks while desperately seeking an opening in her defenses. Every muscle in my body screamed with exhaustion, but I refused to give in. This was it – the moment that would decide the fate of Wonderland and everyone I loved.

As our blades continued to clash, each strike more vicious than the last, I knew I had to end this—one way or another.

The tip of her blade bounced off my armor and I stumbled backwards, nearly losing my grip on the Vorpal Sword. I slipped in the mud and landed flat on my back. My arms flew up to block my face, but it was too late.

Roxanne knelt over me, pressing the tip of her sword into my neck. I felt the buzz of electricity and magic flowing through the metal blade where it made contact with my skin.

I swallowed hard, doing all I could to stay calm.

"Surrender now, and I will make your death quick."

My pulse quickened, but I refused to let fear show on my face. I gritted my teeth against the urge to wipe that self-satisfied look off her face. Squaring my shoulders, I met her gaze defiantly.

"I will *never* surrender to you. I guess you'll just have to kill me slowly."

A groan of disappointment escaped Roxanne's lips as she frowned at me. In that moment of weakness, a narrow flash of black muscle and fangs shot out from my right arm, striking her on the cheek before retreating.

Two small dots of blood welled up on her cheek. Roxanne's hand flew up to the poisonous snake bite. For a moment, surprise flickered in her eyes.

Then, her expression twisted into one of pure rage.

"No!" she gasped, sinking to her hands and knees. The veins in her face began to turn black with Jasmine's poisonous venom, weakening her body, and hopefully, her magic. "What have you done?"

I blinked in surprise before feeling the sensation of my snake tattoo curling her smooth scales around my arm. When I glanced down, she flicked her black forked tongue at me and then disappeared under my armor.

It was exactly the assist that I needed.

Climbing onto my feet, I steadied myself and gripped the Vorpal Sword tighter, summoning what little magic I had left. The sword glowed in response, empowered by my will.

Amari's last words echoed in my mind.

My sister is dead. Kill whatever is left of her . . . Do it for me . . . for Wonderland . . .

With a shaky breath, I braced myself for the gruesome task ahead. Then I raised my sword.

The Red Queen glared at me, her red eyes gleaming with malevolence.

"Do it, little girl," she goaded. "Show me the power you've been so desperate to unleash!"

I clenched my jaw, adrenaline pumping through my veins as I raised the Vorpal Sword over my head. In my mind, I pictured the countless innocent lives she'd taken, the families she'd destroyed, and the chaos she'd sown throughout Wonderland. I reminded myself that this was for the greater good.

"For Wonderland," I whispered, and swung with all my might, knowing that I had to make it count.

The Vorpal Sword plunged into the ground just left of her chest.

"If you surrender, I might be able to convince everyone to spare your life." I yanked the blade out of the bloody gravel and ran it along the Red Queen's neck. Black veins pulsed with poison. "Hand over the Heart of Wonderland, and we'll call it good."

"Never!" she screamed, her magic flaring around her like a dark storm. "You will regret ever setting foot in Wonderland!"

Before I could make contact with her, a red blast of magic threw me backwards. I crashed into the stone wall of the courtyard, the impact driving the breath from my lungs, and possibly breaking a few ribs. As I slumped to the ground, Roxanne sheathed her sword.

"You are wasting my time!" she growled as if she was annoyed. Catching my breath, I could only watch as she stepped back and lifted her hands to the sky. Fiery bolts of red magic sparked out of her fingertips as she cast some kind of summoning spell through the acrid smoke.

I gritted my teeth against the pain in my side, in my shoulder, and now in my ribs. Fighting back tears, I pushed myself up, clutching at the wall for support.

Whatever she was up to, I didn't trust the bitch one bit.

Turns out, I was right not to trust her.

My blood ran cold as an ear-splitting screech tore through the air above us. A wide, twisted grin spread across the Red Queen's face.

"If you won't yield to me, perhaps the Jabberwocky will make you see reason!"

The smoky air swirled as the monstrous creature descended on the military fort. Its massive wings cast huge dark shadows over the large courtyard. Its razor-sharp claws gleamed in the firelight, and I knew that one swipe from the beast would be enough to end me.

"Jabberwocky! Attack!" Roxanne screamed at the demon, her voice twisted with rage. "Kill her!"

The giant demon soared through the air, unscathed by the arrows that bounced off his armor-like scales. My heart leaped into my throat, but I stood firm. The truth was that I was literally up against a wall. I had nowhere else to go.

I watched in terror as the Jabberwocky swooped down around Roxanne and me with terrifying speed, its massive wings sending gusts of wind that threatened to knock us off our feet. Its fiery breath singed the smoky air around us, but it never made contact.

"Damn you! Do as I command!" Roxanne screamed in frustration, her eyes darting between the Jabberwocky and me. Her anger was palpable, a dark storm cloud ready to unleash its wrath upon us all.

"Obey me! Kill Alice!"

The creature's fierce eyes held a hint of defiance, and it circled around again. Instead of attacking me, the creature zipped above us without making a move.

"Destroy her!" Roxanne shrieked, pointing at me with her sword. "Rip her to shreds! Burn her to ash! Leave nothing but bones!"

The Red Queen's fury had clearly reached new heights. The Jabberwocky seemed torn, caught between its loyalty to her and some unknown force that held it back.

I couldn't help but feel a small spark of hope.

"Jabberwocky!" Roxanne screamed again, desperation clawing at her voice. "Kill her! Kill Alice *now*!"

Wincing in pain, I tensed, ready to dodge the beast's attack. But instead of lunging at me as ordered, the Jabberwocky reared up and stepped between us, its massive form casting a shadow over us both.

Meanwhile, the sounds of swords clashing all around me had stopped. All I could hear was the sound of my heart thundering in my ears, and the deep huff of the Jabberwocky's breath.

"Wh-what are you doing?" Roxanne stammered, her fear palpable. "I am your master! You must obey me!"

The Jabberwocky met her gaze with an almost human-like intelligence.

"Looks like your pet demon isn't so loyal after all," I said, smirking despite the pain and the fear that gripped me. "Maybe if you'd been paying attention, you would've noticed that I took off its collar."

The Jabberwocky growled, but it kept its eyes pinned on the Red Queen.

"Very well, Alice," she spat. Even though she was poisoned, her magic began to gather in her hands and crackle like bolts of red lighting. "I'll destroy you myself if I have to!"

She screamed in fury, hurling the deadly bolts towards me.

With a mighty roar, the Jabberwocky opened its massive jaws and unleashed a torrent of flames that collided with the red magic in midair. The explosion of fire shook the ground beneath my feet, pushing against the magic until the Red Queen was completely engulfed in a raging inferno.

Her screams were the sound of nightmares, high-pitched wails that split the air as she writhed in agony.

But it was a nightmare she'd brought onto herself.

Her screams were drowned out by the sound of the crackling fire. Within a few minutes, her body was consumed by the intense heat. I could only watch, numb with shock, as the psychotic terror who had caused so much pain and suffering was reduced to a pile of ashes on the muddy ground.

The Jabberwocky turned to look at me, and I swear we shared a moment.

"Thank you," I said, eternally grateful to this strange, misunderstood creature. Then it flapped its wings, clearing the smoke out of the courtyard, before taking to the sky. It disappeared in the moonlight like a phantom.

I stood there, panting and shaking, staring at the pile of ashes that used to be the Red Queen. A soft, pulsing red glow caught my eye.

The Heart of Wonderland.

Just like the Jabberwocky, it was whole. And it was free.

Its power seemed to call out to me, whispering promises of a new era where peace and balance would finally reign over Wonderland. I immediately knelt down to take the Heart into my trembling hands.

I could feel its warmth and energy surge throughout my body. I felt the cut in my shoulder start to heal in record speed, along with my broken ribs. My muscles stopped aching, and my feet didn't hurt.

As I lifted it high, cheers erupted from our soldiers, their voices carrying across the battlefield like a triumphant song. I looked around the courtyard and saw that every last soldier from the Red Army had laid down their weapons and surrendered to the White Knight.

"Take them prisoner—for now," Jack ordered, his voice firm but fair. "They've been misled by the Red Queen long enough. It's time for them to learn what true leadership looks like."

I spotted Callister and Hatter coming towards me, followed by Chess.

"Is it...is it over?" I asked, my voice barely above a whisper.

Chess grinned, his brilliant green eyes shining with pride. "It's over, Alice. For the first time in centuries, Wonderland is free from the Red Queen's tyranny."

More cheers erupted from the soldiers who had fought valiantly by our side, and I nearly dropped the Heart on the ground when I saw Ransom emerge from the fortress with Queen Amari in his arms.

I ran over to her, thrilled to find her still alive. The soldiers were cheering and shouting so loud that I could hardly hear her over the noise.

"You did it," she said with a labored breath. "Alice . . . you did it."

"So did you!" I cried in disbelief. "How are you not dead?"

She shook her head weakly, and the look in Ransom's eyes told me that her prognosis was bad.

"I don't have much time left . . . but I wanted to thank you for saving our realm."

I blinked, refusing to believe that this was the end for her.

After spending an eternity battling the inherent evil of her sisters, Amari deserved so much more.

"Take this," I said, shoving the Heart against the bandages on her chest. "If it can heal me, it can heal you."

"Alice . . . I can't . . . " she tried to protest, but I wasn't having it.

"Yeah, you can. Let it do its healing thing, and then we'll send someone who's not human to go put it back where it belongs. I pinky swear."

Amari gave me a curious look.

"What is pinky swear?"

"It's a promise," I explained, offering her my pinky. In her lightheaded daze, she didn't quite grasp the concept, so I gently took her hand and hooked my pinky around hers. "As soon as you're better, we're putting the Heart of Wonderland back where it belongs. Who wants the job?"

I looked around at my inhuman wicked boys, knowing they were probably the most eligible candidates.

"Ransom . . . " said Amari, looking up at him with approval. She patted his arm, motioning for him to set her down. The light in her eyes was brighter, and there was more color in her cheeks. "Ransom should take it. And bring Chess with you. Make sure you hide it well. I never want to see it again."

"It would be an honor, Your Majesty," Ransom

said with a polite bow. "When would you like us to go?"

"As soon as I'm fully healed," she replied. "There is much to do, and I can't do it alone."

Dawn was approaching, and the puffy pale clouds stretching across the sky were tinged blue and purple. It felt like every living creature in Wonderland was waiting for the sun.

Every creature except one.

Jack walked up to me, his platinum hair matted with sweat and blood. He pulled me close, and I sank into the sensation of his arms around me. When I looked up, he was studying me with a mixture of admiration and concern.

"You were brilliant out there," he said softly. "Braver than I could have ever asked for."

"You were pretty spectacular yourself."

"Are you hurt?"

I shook my head, feeling oddly fine after the adrenaline-fueled bloodbath. "No, I'm alright. Just...tired."

"Understandable," Hatter chimed in, his mismatched eyes twinkling with mirth despite the grim scene around us. "It's not every day one saves an entire realm from destruction."

"That's true," I agreed, glancing around at the shattered landscape and the countless bodies that littered the ground. "Jack," I said hesitantly, "what do we do now?"

He caressed my hair with a gentle hand, his

touch strong and reassuring. His smile was slow and sweet. "Now, we rebuild. Together."

His hand found mine, twining our fingers. Tears pricked my eyes as I squeezed his hand.

"You mean that?"

Jack lifted an eyebrow. He motioned to where Hatter and Callister were standing. Then he pointed at Chess and Ransom. "Do you think any of them will want you to leave? You belong here, Alice. You belong with us . . . with the people who love you the most."

Warmth flooded through my body, knowing I was loved. Not just by Jack, but by *all* of my wicked boys of Wonderland. I wrapped my arms around him and was about to kiss him, but the moment was interrupted by Hatter debating with Queen Amari.

"I know it has to be done, but *look* at this place . . . " Hatter motioned to the rot and the mud surrounding us, and the piles of mangled bodies that some of the soldiers were starting to load into carts. "Even after Ransom and Chess return the Heart of Wonderland to where it belongs, it's going to take a *lot* of work to repair the damage your sister did."

"Then let us begin that work together," Amari replied, her voice ringing clear and strong. I could tell that the Heart of Wonderland was working its magic on her injuries. "Alice, come with me. We need to address our people."

Our people?

Before I could ask what that was all about, the

White Queen took my hand and led me up the pile of stones and rubble from the collapsed fortress wall. A round of cheers erupted from the soldiers. She waited until we both reached the top, then held up the perfectly intact Heart of Wonderland. More cheers and shouts echoed off the walls. The sound was nearly deafening.

I looked down at Chess, Callister, Hatter, Ransom, and Jack, along with the countless others who had fought alongside me...alongside *us*. Their faces were bloody and weary, but their eyes shone with hope and determination.

Amari began to speak, her voice steady despite the massive injury she was recovering from. "Today is a new beginning for Wonderland. Together, we will forge a new path for our people—a world free from hatred and darkness. A world where the Kingdom of Diamonds and Ice is in balance with the Kingdom of Hearts and Roses. A world where Wonderland's two queens can exist in harmony. With that being said, it's time to vote for the next Red Queen!"

"Alice! Alice!" the soldiers cheered, raising their swords in salute to me. The vote was unanimous. Everyone with a voice was shouting my name.

I should've been happy, but the more they began to chant, the more I began to panic at the thought of becoming the next Red Queen.

"Amari, I'm flattered, but I can't be the next Red Queen," I told her.

She blinked as if she didn't understand.

"Why not? Alice . . . you have earned this honor. Everyone loves you. You saved Wonderland. You saved the very Heart of Wonderland. And you did it without being the one to kill my sister . . . or her Jabberwocky. Do you not want to stay in Wonderland?"

I tried to think about my old life in Los Angeles. The parties, the drugs, the fake friends, and the emptiness. It all seemed like a distant dream now. Wonderland had become real to me.

For the first time in my life, I felt like I truly belonged.

But to be the Red Queen?

Hard pass.

"I can't do it," I said with a reluctant shrug. I felt a warmth near my side, and turned to see the Cheshire Cat hovering near me.

"What seems to be the problem?" he crooned by my ear.

"Alice doesn't want to be the next Red Queen," Amari explained.

Chess frowned in confusion.

"But you deserve to be one of our queens. We love you, Alice. Do you not wish to stay here with us?"

"I do," I said quickly. "I wanna stay with all of you. And maybe I could even be a leader . . . but the Red Queen? I don't want to have *anything* to do with Roxanne's legacy. I don't want—" I stopped myself short, afraid that I was asking for too much.

"It's alright, Alice," Queen Amari said with a reassuring smile. "Tell us what you want."

I scanned the joyful faces of the crowd

surrounding us. Then I looked at Chess and Amari. "I don't want to be called the Red Queen."

The Cheshire Cat narrowed his eyes, deep in thought. "So . . . it's the title, then?"

By now, Ransom, Jack, Hatter, and Callister had joined us, trying to sort out the details.

"It's also the location," I added. "If I stay here, I don't want to live in Roxanne's moldy, run-down shit-hole far away from Amari. I'd rather be neighbors with her."

"I see . . . " Chess mused. "So, you'd like a new castle and a title that is something different than the Red Queen?"

"Yeah."

"We can build you a castle," Hatter said with a wink. "That's easy."

"But what title would be best?" Callister chimed in. He lit a pumpkin spice latte-flavored cigarette and sucked in a lungful of sweetness.

"The Sexy Queen?" Hatter replied.

"No," I laughed.

"The Tattooed Queen?" Callister suggested.

"It sounds like false advertising," I shrugged. "I've only got the one."

"Yes, but you can always get more."

"I know your title," Ransom declared, digging into his pocket. He took out a deck of cards and fanned them out. "Pick a card. Whatever it is will be your new title."

I shot him a smirk.

"I don't know. I've played this game with you

before. What happens if I pull the four of spades, or the six of diamonds?"

Ransom laughed. While it was wicked, it was also sincere.

"Do you trust me, Alice?"

"Yeah."

"Then pick a card. Any card will do."

I bit my lip, even though it was my king's job, and I started to tug one of the cards from his hand.

But it didn't feel right.

I quickly tucked it back into place. I carefully teased out the one next to it instead.

That one felt right.

When I looked at it, I grinned like a Cheshire Cat. I couldn't stop smiling.

My eyes flicked up to Ransom, who was grinning just as wide.

"What card did you pull?" Callister demanded.

"Yes, which one is it?" Hatter asked.

Chess purred with interest. "Show us!"

I rolled my eyes, still smiling at Ransom. "There's no way this is legit. Turn your cards over."

He shook his head.

"I'll show you mine if you show me yours."

"Fine, then we'll do it at the same time. Ready?"

"Ready."

We both revealed our cards. Ransom had a full deck spread out, minus the one card that was in my hand.

"Well?" asked Jack, leaning closer to me. "What's your new title?"

I lifted up the card, and Amari nodded in approval.

"Attention, everyone!" she shouted, and we waited for the crowd to hush long enough for her to say my new name.

"It is my great honor to officially introduce you to Alice, the Queen of Hearts!"

A roar of approval rose from the crowd, their cheers thundering through the frosty air. I felt a massive wave of emotion well up inside me, causing tears of happiness that threatened to spill over. For the first time in my life, I was being accepted for who I *truly* was, and I was being celebrated for it.

I turned to Jack, who was wearing an expression of pure pride. He reached out to brush the tears from my cheeks with his thumbs, then cradled the back of my head in his hands. He looked into my eyes with a tenderness that verged on reverence. The crowd's noise faded into the background as I held his gaze.

"The title suits you well," he murmured before brushing his cool lips against mine. "I hereby pledge my fealty to the Queen of Hearts. Long may she reign."

Pssst . . .
I need your opinion. Got a sec?

Leaving reviews is one of the most kickass ways to support authors. You're also helping other readers decide if our books are right for them. If you have a minute, I'd LOVE a review from you!

Review Queen of Hearts on Amazon

Thanks so much!

Jekka

JEKKA'S WILDE ONES

Desperate for more?

Join Jekka's Wilde Ones!

Get immediate access to Jekka's private Facebook group, character art, the spiciest new Fantasy & PNR books, and be notified of new releases, bonus epilogues, and exclusive novellas before anyone else.

Become a Wilde One at jekkawilde.com/ newsletter

ABOUT THE AUTHOR

Jekka Wilde (aka the Duchess of Depravity) reigns supreme in her frostbitten kingdom in the northern US, where she's practically *forced* to write steamy stories to stay warm.

A self-proclaimed caffeine aficionado, she can often be found snuggled under a blanket fortress, sipping a matcha latte that's almost as hot as the scorching scenes in her books.

In a house that's part library, part shoe warehouse, Jekka's motto in life and literature is 'Why Choose?'—a philosophy that's evident in every romance she writes. The only thing filthier than her humor is the plot.

If you're looking for sweet romance, keep walking. But if you're ready for a wild, witty, and wicked ride, congratulations!

You've just found your new favorite author.

Made in the USA
Coppell, TX
02 November 2024

39518691R00173